QUEER LIFE,
QUEER LOVE

QUEER LIFE, QUEER LOVE 2

Edited by Matt Bates
and Julia Bell

MUSWELL
PRESS

First published by Muswell Press in 2023
Introduction copyright © Matt Bates and Julia Bell 2023
The moral right of each contributor to be identified as the Author
of their work has been asserted by them in accordance
with the Copyright, Designs, and Patents Act 1988

Typeset in Bembo by M Rules
Printed and bound by CPI Group (UK) Ltd, Croydon, CR0 4YY

A CIP catalogue record for this book is available from the British Library

ISBN: 978-1-73912-382-6
eISBN: 978-1-73912-383-3

Muswell Press
London N6 5HQ
www.muswell-press.co.uk

Printed and bound in the UK on FSC® certified paper in line with our continuing
commitment to ethical business practices, sustainability and the environment.
For further information see faber.co.uk/environmental-policy

Contents

Introduction: In Our Own Words

In his *TLS* review for the first *Queer Life, Queer Love* anthology, Kevin Brazil observed that the subject of sex was 'notably absent from many texts', suggesting 'a shift from a previous generation of queer writing, and an expansion of what [queer] love might be'.[*]

Brazil is right. The sexual revolutions of the 1960s and '70s allowed queer writers to speak more explicitly about sex, a trend which persisted through the queer publishing boom of the 1980s and '90s, when writers deliberately and provocatively positioned gay sex at the forefront of their work, relishing their prescribed deviancy. Describing, documenting, and celebrating sex was vital to resisting the narratives of compulsory heterosexuality which threatened to erase and negate queer experiences of desire. These narrations were a form of radical defiance to ensure visibility in the face of social discrimination, homophobia, Clause 28 and the devastating AIDS crisis.

So, what does it mean to be queer in 2023 and what are

---

[*]   Brazil, Kevin, 'How Good It Felt', *Times Literary Supplement*, March 2022.

the some of the issues we are concerned with? Judging by many of the entries published in this anthology it would appear that new modes of queer relations, particularly those built around the subject of friendship, are central concerns. We read of friendships under pressure; friendships that could-have-been or fail to meet expectations; friendships grieved over or regretted; and friendships that, literally, become undressed. This engagement with 'friendship' chimes with some of the ideas that Michel Foucault floated in his 1981 interview, 'Friendship as a Way of Life'. Foucault suggested that rather than grounding queer subjectivities solely within the confines of sexuality and desire, we might do better by reaching for new 'relations' through our queerness. 'The problem is not to discover in oneself the truth of one's sex', he writes, but, rather, 'to use one's sexuality henceforth to arrive at a multiplicity of relationships'. For Foucault, this is the reason why queerness is not simply 'a form of desire' but, rather, a mode of living, something 'desirable' in itself. Queer culture, he implies, has the capacity both culturally and socially to produce real societal change and is just as relevant to the disaffected heterosexual as it is to queers.*

Writing from a queer perspective in 2023, then, is about far more than what happens in bed; it's also, as Foucault notes, about what we do with our time. About whom we choose to spend our time with and relate to, about our sense of ourselves in the world. Queerness is about a refusal and an inability to fit into a box marked 'normal', and its expression is often a deliberate re-conceptualisation of

---

* Foucault, Michel, *Ethics: Essential Works 1954–84*, trans. by Robert Hurley, (London: Penguin, 2020).

gender, chafing against the stereotypes that would put all of us into rigid categories. Queer words are an opportunity to consider and recover how we navigate our often-difficult relationships with friends and families. A point reiterated by J. Halberstam in *The Queer Art of Failure*. Here, the 'queer version' of 'selfhood' is one 'that depends upon disconnection from the family', and its 'contingent relations to friends and improved relations to community'.* These kinds of creative relationships can offer new, capacious ways of living. The reinvention of the family begins in the art forms that express the queer worlds we inhabit, which are full of grand-dandies, gender-fluid teenagers, trans men and women, lesbians, gay men and all the points of the compass in between from hypersexual to sapiosexual to asexual.

Published in the same week as this introduction is being written, the 2021 census included data on sexual orientation for the first time. The report estimates that just over three percent of the population in England and Wales aged sixteen and over identified as LGBT+, an almost doubling in number from 2014.† Queer living demonstrates alternative, resilient ways of being, offering a successful model on how to live, manage, and thrive in difficult, liminal spaces through the cultivation of the queer collective which expands the traditional family structures. When we create our own queer families and break free of our genealogical ties, or, alternatively, look for creative ways to assert/insert the validity of queerness within those traditional family

* Halberstam, Judith, *The Queer Art of Failure*, (Durham and London: Duke University Press, 2011).

† 'Sexual orientation, England and Wales: Census 2021' Office for National Statistics. Accessed Online: https://www.ons.gov.uk/peoplepopulationandcommunity/culturalidentity/sexuality/bulletins/sexualorientationenglandandwales/census2021

constructs, we edge ever closer to a queer utopia. The prospect is neither assimilation nor alienation, but, rather, a freer way of living, overcoming oppression, and founded upon equality, honesty, respect, and compassion. Perhaps that is why there is higher identification with being queer right now, as the census would suggest.

We had an overwhelming response to the *Queer Life, Queer Love* call out for this second anthology and, inevitably, have only been able to feature a relatively small number of the works submitted. We thank all of those who submitted for sharing and trusting their words with us. We believe that the stories and poems that are presented here offer a rich, wide and diverse selection of not just the themes and preoccupations of queers today but also different approaches to writing queer words. The anthology reflects the subjectivities of queer lives, wrestles with their construct and marginalisation, and attempts to articulate those spaces – both domestic and social – from which they operate. Now, more than ever, it is imperative that the LGBTQI+ community stands together. Both nationally and globally queer lives continue to be marginalised, oppressed, and erased. We are always stronger together.

Julia Bell and Matt Bates
February 2023

Old Queen as Ecosystem –
Nathan Evans

I grew up
between hard heart and rock
of family and school   law and bible
each root downed   nourishment found
was stake upon an even ground
each florid frond a win over winds
changing tune in lento tempo to relative major
now old but bold   bent but unbowed
I have made myself home
to multiple organisms   Bois buzz blossoms
palating first pollen   Fetishists feather–up
in leafy locker rooms   Twinks sing old favourites
over newfangled twig percussion   Polyamorists branch out
Jocks bough up   Monogamists nest in nooks   Otters strip
bark to build designer dens with Geek boyfriends   Pups lick
sap and low-hanging Daddies toss rewards to them
Bears winter
in my trunk's
hollow centre
spooned around
Cubs and Chasers
Pigs rut roots for musky delicacies
Queers party in underground arches   Discreets bury
histories   Trans migrate microclimates
are one with all of us

Nathan Evans' poetry has been published by *Queerlings*, Dead Ink, *Impossible Archetype*, Manchester Metropolitan University and Untitled. His first collection, *Threads*, was longlisted for the Polari First Book Prize; his second collection, *CNUT*, is published by Inkandescent. He was longlisted for the 2020 Live Canon Poetry Competition, hosts BOLD Queer Poetry Soirée and is a member of King's Poets.

Can't We Be Friends? –
Avi Ben-Zeev

No way, Justin on OkCupid likes me! The Justin? Justin, Justin?

All this San Francisco talk about asking the universe for personal favours and manifesting reality, as though our puny existence means anything cosmic. I've found it arrogant, at best, but wait ... is Justin's *like* kismet or what?

Compatibility can't be reduced to a list, so why even bother reading his stats? Besides, I know them.

Or do I?

What if I find out something new? A deal breaker? Like if he's taken up smoking or gone vegan. But who am I kidding? Nothing would be a dealbreaker, not when it comes to Justin.

Justin
43 • San Francisco
Man | Gay | Top | Versatile | Monogamous | Single
180 cm | Athletic Build
Black | Agnostic | Pisces | Liberal | Self-employed
Vegan | Doesn't smoke cigarettes | Drinks
sometimes

I deep-dive into his selfie's brown eyes, lingering without needing air. *Swipe.* Justin with his arm around a woman. A woman? Must be a friend. *Swipe.* Damn, a half-naked beach photo? For years, I've fantasised about taking his shirt off and running my fingers on his chiselled chest, but this is too WHAM. I want – *gasp, gasp, gasp* – an old-fashioned undressing, a slow reveal.

So, what now? Like him back? Write him?

Ping. A message appears in my OkCupid mailbox. It's from Justin; of course it is.

I can't read it. Not yet.

What if he recognised me? No, it's impossible; how could he have connected the dots? It's been what? Seven years? Besides, Justin knew *her*, Talia, the over-the-top glittery straight femme, not me, Avi, the rugged gay bear. I look nothing like my all-too-passing drag-queen past, my pre-gender-transition incarnation.

The me I've come to trust is decisive, but my gut screams opposite directives.

Click and read.

Delete without reading.

As if I could do both at the same time.

It's better to leave myths as myths, right? Impossibilities as impossibilities? I crave truth, and I'd do almost anything for a romantic adventure with him, the one-and-only Justin, but—

Ahhhhhhhh,

my fingers are paralysed.

*

In 2001 and at the age of thirty-six, Talia arrived in San Francisco in a full-blown existential crisis and dire need of a haircut. Her rainbow-coloured, Samson-like locks had grown into an oversized shield.

Talia didn't always look this way – a glorious hyper-feminine extravaganza of poodley faux-fur jackets, pinup-style swing dresses, and platform heels so high she was walking a tightrope. As a kid, Talia sat with her legs too wide apart for a girl – at least that's what our elementary teacher had said – and cut her hair as close to her scalp as Mom's rusty kitchen scissors allowed. Then, in an outburst of inspiration or vengeance, she gave buzzcuts to our Barbie dolls too.

'I'm a boy,' she'd protest when adults would tell her what a pretty girl she was and what a shame about her hair. Why couldn't they have seen that?

Our new neighbour on 22nd near Castro offered a local's tip: 'Honey, there's only one person in the whole San Francisco Bay Area that will do your hair justice. Justin, On Mars. Let me tell you, he's a spiritual guy, a shaman of sorts, so an appointment with him will be transformative.'

The City by the Bay offered a place for reinvention. People came here to find themselves, techies excepted. So, a shamanic hairdresser? Why not?

Early, as per usual, Talia peered through the salon's front window. Was that Justin, the striking guy with the mohawk dreads? It had to be Justin! He was the only man in a gaggle of tattooed hipster women, and what a sight – his square glasses lent a bookish librarian sensibility to his otherwise edgy appearance, and his muscles rippled from a tight T-shirt.

She,

I,

. . . fell in love at first sight. The way Justin moved? This wasn't the stuff of words. Sunsets are cliched until they aren't. Or maybe Talia didn't desire Justin as much as she wanted to become him. With hindsight's lens, only precious few morsels can be recovered as truth.

'What brings you to our fair city?' It could have been a nicety, but Justin sounded sincere.

'I'm searching for home,' Talia said.

'Is home a place?' Justin dug his fingers into her unruly mane and massaged her scalp. His touch tingled her spine and exposed a tightness in her forehead.

On the counter, by the various styling products and other hairdressing paraphernalia, was a framed photograph of Justin with African tribal make-up.

Talia stuck her hand outside the gown and pointed. 'My neighbour called you a shaman.'

Justin grinned. 'Oh, that? It's for Halloween.' He combed her hair and snipped the ends. 'Your neighbour, is she a white lady?'

'Yeah, probably.' It wasn't always straightforward. Some light-skinned people, like herself, were mixed-race.

'Then I'd venture to say she's fetishising Black people as being magic.'

'Deification as othering?'

'Yup.' Justin kept combing and snip, snip, snipping. 'What do you do for a living?'

'I'm a psychology professor.'

'Oh no, you're the one with the superpowers to read people's minds.' He winked. 'I need to be careful of what I say from now on.'

'Don't worry, I'm a researcher, not a therapist. Besides, it's too late.'

'Oh, yeah, and what's the verdict, professor?'

'At the risk of projecting, you have an artist's soul.'

Every six weeks, Justin indulged Talia's punky aesthetic, but *beauty, shmeuty*; seeing Justin was the real reason she kept coming back. Safer topics like books and movies soon morphed into confessionals.

'I sometimes feel ashamed of being a hairstylist,' Justin said, adding green streaks to Talia's multi-coloured curls. He had stayed after hours to accommodate her schedule, or so he said.

'How come?' Talia's voice betrayed her surprise.

'I was the first in my family to go to college. Stanford, if you can believe it.' He shook his head. 'But I fucked up.'

'What happened?'

'My freshman year was rough. I felt too self-conscious to speak in class and drew blanks on homework and exams. But in my second year, a history professor I admired took me under his wing. He told me I had talent.' Justin's hands trembled as he grabbed a section of Talia's hair and placed a foil underneath. 'I joined his research team, felt like I finally found my calling, but then . . .'

'You bolted?'

'I did. I packed my stuff and left. The irony is that I idolised this man so much I was afraid of disappointing him. What a joke.'

'It sounds like you're being too harsh on yourself, dear man.' Filled with emotion, the rest of her words got garbled in her gut. 'I've been on that calling-it-quits edge more than once.'

Justin tilted his head. 'But you have a Ph.D.'

'I grew up in a working-class Israeli town, failed

arithmetic in the third grade, and get this, got kicked out of my elementary-school choir.'

'Now, that's cruel and unusual.'

'I know; who does that to a kid?' Talia smiled. It wasn't funny, but it was. 'Imagine this horror show – a class of forty restless kids trapped in 40 degrees Celsius, no aircon, with one window facing the town cemetery.'

Justin laughed, and the brush fell to the floor, leaving a green smudge. 'Sorry, go on.'

'Nobody expected us to go to college, and I all but failed high school, but against all odds, I did get into university. The moment I started caring about doing well, I freaked.'

'Yup, sounds familiar.' Justin scrubbed the floor with a rag and slapped on a new pair of latex gloves.

'I didn't realise it at the time, but my worry had a name, *stereotype threat*. People 'like me' weren't supposed to occupy intellectual spaces, so even the smallest failure risked proving I didn't belong. So yeah, I packed my bags too. Several times.'

'How did you end up sticking with it?'

'Unexpected allies and imaginary conversations with my beloved dead grandmother who had escaped Jewish lynching in Russia. But how about I save this story for next time?' Talia admired Justin's creation. The fresh highlights snaking from her head were a work of art.

'Six weeks is a long time to wait.' Justin opened his arms for a hug, but Talia's breasts got in the way of surrendering to his touch.

Living six weeks to six weeks was unbearable, but when Justin offered to get coffee or hit the town, Talia made excuses for why she couldn't. Keeping a container felt important, and eventually, he stopped trying.

And just like that, a year flew by, and Halloween was once again around the corner. Talia immersed herself in Stephen King's universe. Justin was a horror fan, and she needed to catch up.

On Halloween eve, she waltzed into On Mars with a giddy expression, grabbed a pair of scissors, and waved them about. 'How about *you* sit in the chair today?'

Justin giggled like a school kid. 'You're freaking me out.'

'But, *I'm your number one fan,*' Talia tried for her best Kathy Bates' *Misery* impression, and they laughed so hard, they wet their faces.

'I have news to share, ready?' She waited for Justin to drape the plastic cape over her latest outfit – a pink sequin jumpsuit from The Piedmont Boutique. 'I met this guy online, and he's flying over from Boston for the weekend for our first date.'

Hmmm, Justin muttered, mixing red and purple dyes with who knows what and filling the room with an acrid smell.

'The thing is . . . he's a transgender man.'

'A trans guy, really?'

'I didn't know it was possible,' Talia whispered. Perhaps my past incarnation should have tried harder to see me, but language is crucial for possibilities, is it not? 'I'm excited to meet him, but I've been having all these dreams, night-mares really; it's like something deep inside me has been triggered, and—'

'You shouldn't force yourself to do something you're uncomfortable with.'

'I'm not.' She tried taking a deep breath, but her nose was clogged. Had Justin used a different, more noxious chemical this time? 'Would *you* date a transgender man?'

'If I'm honest, no, I wouldn't.'

'How come?' Talia did and didn't want to know.

'I'm attracted to men, real men.'

They spent the rest of the time in silence, listening to *Ella & Louis*. Justin didn't know it, but this album was one of Talia's favourites growing up, a lucky find at a vinyl record store in Tel Aviv that had helped her escape an oppressive existence. Eyes shut, she hummed along to one of its sadder songs, 'Can't We be Friends?' Why was heartbreak so damn inevitable? And how had Justin's soothing touch turned painful?

That weekend everything changed. Talia made love to the trans man from Boston and stared into a rebirthing mirror. There I knelt, Avi, the boy, now man, begging to be freed. Naked and shivering, I held my new-born self like a father would, rocking back and forth.

Elated, petrified, seized by the future's uncertainty, I didn't know much, but this I did know – the only way forward was to mature into who I had always been.

*

The cold, hard truth is that Talia, no, *I* ghosted Justin. I refuse to rationalise why. I feel guilty, and I should. And, no, I still haven't read his OkCupid message, but I haven't deleted it either.

It's time, yes? My heart whooshing in my ears, I hover my finger over the keyboard and . . . *click.*

Hi, Avi!
Love what you wrote, and you're very handsome.
I'm a big believer in honesty, so I'll be upfront. I
accept trans guys 100%, but I could never date one.

I realize you're looking for romance, but can't we
be friends?
-Justin

Friends? Really? Fuck you, Justin. Fuck you and the horse
you rode in on. Clicking and clacking, I bang a response
like a man possessed. *How would you feel if a guy on a dating
app explained that he would befriend but not date Black men?* But
I don't send it. There's a difference between rejecting some-
one as lover material based on race versus assumed body
parts, right? Or at least I think there is, and I'm fuming, but
under the anger, I sense a lava-like hurt, and I don't want
to pile harm upon harm.

Justin's too precious for that.

I want to be better than that.

Breathe, just breathe.

Dear Justin,
You're my type, too, more than you know. But
like you said, I'm on this platform to date, so I
respectfully decline your friendship offer.
I'm tempted to stop here. Perhaps I should,
but I'll add this — how could I be friends with a
gay man who makes such a sweeping declaration
about not dating trans men? No trans guy in the
whole wide world, ever? If it's about dick size, well,
some trans men have had bottom surgery. If not,
what then?
It'd be too painful to be friends, especially
because you're such an open-hearted and caring
person. Don't ask me how I know, but I do.
I wish you much happiness with whatever you

15

do next with *your one wild and precious life*, as the
poet Mary Oliver so urgently put it.

And love, I wish you love.

Avi

P.S. I know I sound sanctimonious but trust
me, I have regrets about getting stuck in my own
fears and limitations and inflicting harm without
intending to. That famous road to hell ...

I was hoping for closure, but no, my mind is a bully. Why
didn't I write Justin a more vulnerable note? What hijacks
my heart from living life to the fullest? And quoting Mary
Oliver? Yeah, right. I'm such a hypocrite!

Ping.

Hello again, dear Avi,

It took my therapist to point out something I
wasn't ready to admit. I'm scared of what I don't
know. How do I pleasure a trans man? And what if
I'm attracted to him, but when he takes his clothes
off, his body doesn't turn me on? The last thing I'd
want is to offend him.

Then again, if we were to go there and sex
went south, who am I to be your caretaker? I'm
sure you can and do take care of yourself. My
intentions were good, but I'd understand if what I
wrote felt condescending. Yup, that good ol' road
to hell!

There's something else. I didn't finish my
undergrad, and I'm worried I won't measure up to
a psychology professor. I had a client once, a good

friend, who was also a psych prof, but one day, she disappeared. But I'm digressing. Sorry.

Meet up for a drink at Martuni's tonight? My treat.

-Justin

Martuni's is a San Francisco institution – a gay piano bar with dim lighting, ambient music, and a vast selection of strong and colourful Martinis. The perfect spot for a date.

I'm usually the first to arrive, but Justin has beaten me to it. He's at the bar, heartbreakingly handsome, the new lines on his face softened by candlelight.

'Hi Avi, I'm Justin.' He offers his hand. 'You look just like your pictures.'

Hey, it's me, I almost say, but instead, I shake his hand. 'Nice to meet you,' I mutter, my throat dry.

'What would you like?' He's holding a neon-green drink garnished with a Granny Smith slice.

I dislike Martinis, but it doesn't matter. 'Whatever you're having,' I say, heat stinging my face. My voice has deepened; I have facial hair, a square jaw, and my body is built, but my eyes – how can he not recognise my eyes?

'Another Apple Sour,' Justin tells the bartender. Turning to me, he says, 'I want to apologise—'

'Please don't; if anyone should apologise, it's me.'

'You?'

'Yes, before we go any further, there's something I need to come clean about. You see, the psychology professor you mentioned—'

'You know her?'

'You can say that.'

Justin's eyes pop. 'Talia? Is that you?'

'Yes, but no,' I say, my voice trembling.

'That's a lot to take in.' He puts his coat on and slams two twenty-dollar bills on the counter. 'Sorry, but I'm outta here.'

I follow him, panting. 'Justin, wait.'

On the corner of Valencia and Market, he turns around, tears gushing down his cheeks. 'I must have left you a million messages asking what happened, and nothing? That's so fucking cruel.'

'You're right. There's no excuse, but please, hear me out.' I don't want to betray him again by twisting the truth to be pretty or palatable. 'Talia, I mean I,' I cough into my hand, 'was foolishly in love with you. The thing is, it was easier to bear when I was a so-called woman. But then, when I finally awakened to what I've known all my life but didn't have the words for – that I was a man, a gay man – to find out you'd reject me no matter what. Well, that was devastating.' There, I said it. 'And I might have been thirty-eight in human years, but in trans years I was an infant, and my skin was brittle. I couldn't face you, face that ultimate rejection. I'm sorry; I really am.'

'In love?'

'Yes.'

'I had feelings for you too, but I didn't know what to do with them. A crush on a woman? It felt like insanity.'

'Would a crush on a drag queen have been more acceptable?'

Justin smiles. 'Yes, definitely,' he says, pulling me close, our chests aligned for the first time. 'Come home with me?'

'I want to, but I'm terrified.' I bury my face in his neck, inhaling his woodsy smell deep into my lungs.

'Me too, but however things go tonight, promise you won't disappear again.'

'I promise,' I say and lean into his kiss. Justin's kiss. The Justin. Justin, Justin.

Avi Ben-Zeev is a gay transgender man, psychology professor, writer, and EDI facilitator, newly living in London, UK. He received a Ph.D. in Cognitive Psychology from Yale University and has been faculty at Brown, Williams College, and San Francisco State University. A recent graduate of Birkbeck's Creative Writing MFA, he is passionate about applying psychological inquiries to memoir and fiction.

Section 28 Coupling –
Kath Gifford

(after Karen McCarthy Woolf, Malika Booker and Margaret Thatcher)

Children who need to be taught
about diversity

to respect
difference

traditional moral values
of love thy neighbour

are being taught
instead to deny or hate,

that they have an inalienable right to be gay
is lost, with an uneducated generation to HIV

All of those children
thrown to the wolves, without freedom to be themselves

are being cheated
of information,

of a sound start in life
and decent dance music, a camp I want to live in

Yes, cheated.

* the lines in italics are from a speech by Margaret Thatcher to the
Conservative Party Conference, Blackpool, 9th October, 1987.

The Blue Boy – Kath Gifford

I painted the Blue Boy statue pink
in Exeter's Princesshay
on the anniversary of Section 28,
then sashay'd away.

I bought red and white paint
in separate shops, my shaved head
and purple quiff too memorable
to be forgotten buying pink.

'Sick Gay Activist'
Proclaimed the *Excess & Error.*
'Traditional Moral Values'
bred shame and suicides.

Not 'intentionally promoting'
'pretended family relationships'
I also painted a black triangle
on his traditional concrete Mum.

Section 28 had blood on its Clause.

Kath Gifford was anthologised in City Lit's *Between the Lines* 2021, 2022, Ripon Poetry Festival 2021, 2022, and *Hot Poets – SPARKS*, December 2022. She is published online by Urban Tree Festival Competition and The RSL Write Across London Poetry Map. Lyric essays about Sarcoidosis at healthandresilience.co.uk and in Wordgathering online journal Summer 2023. The winner of London Lit Lab Queer Competition July 2022, Kath Gifford was shortlisted for The Bridport Prize 2022.

I Want To Suck This Man's Toes –
Adam Zmith

For the past few weeks I've been obsessed with my new flatmate. There's a part of him that's just too mesmerising to resist: the beauty, the shape, and the promise of his feet.

I haven't even seen them bare – only sheathed in the white cotton furry socks he wears every day from a seven-pack. He comes home from work, flops down onto the sofa, and elevates his feet on the sofa arm. The soles of his white socks are grey on the pressure points of his individual toes, the balls, and the heels. Sometimes I'm close enough to smell their musk. I've definitely taken a deep sniff inside his work boots when he's out: a dense aroma, fuzzy and mossy.

One night at the end of the first week of our living together when I came home from work, M. was laid out on the sofa, feet up, texting. I had to sit down at the table across from him just to be close to those feet. I tore open the plastic carton containing the chicken tikka masala that I'd just picked up at the supermarket. I couldn't waste time heating it up. I just sat and ate it opposite M.'s feet while he tapped away on his phone screen.

M.'s schedule runs like clockwork, which is great for me. He displays his two enticing twins to me daily, in this way, at exactly the same time. I'm able to plan to eat my evening meal with a view at just the right moment. It's like eating in the restaurant at Disneyland during the nightly fireworks.

*

'You can leave your shoes here,' M. told me when he opened the door to his flat. I levered my feet out of my trainers and felt like he'd given me permission to look at his socks. We'd only just met. 'I usually keep my socks on at home though,' he added, half-laughing and awkward at the same time.

As I followed him inside M. said, 'To be honest my ex left me in the shit.' He touched a bag of beetroot on the table. I hadn't taken off my coat, because I was only viewing the room. This is how we met – via an ad on a flatshare website.

'I can't cover the rent by myself,' M. explained, watching me look around his flat, 'So I have to get someone in.'

'Yeah, that's cool,' I said, my eyes dropping to the floor, which wasn't as soft as I was expecting. The carpet was pretty thin, same as in the bedroom he pointed to. It ran through most of the flat and had been the colour of cream when laid, I could tell. At some points it didn't quite reach the wall. I kept my hand on the phone in my pocket so I could feel it buzz in case I got a yes from one of my previous viewings, or (more likely) if my next one wanted to cancel.

'I'll clear a shelf in the fridge for whoever takes the room, and there's a whole cupboard here for them.' He stepped onto the kitchen lino which ran along one side of the

open-plan room. He opened the cupboard door to show
the empty space there.

'Right, and . . . erm, what type of flatmate are you look-
ing for?'

'One who pays the rent,' he laughed, then stopped and
toyed with the beetroot in the plastic bag. 'I mean, just
someone chill, really. I like space, I guess?'

'Yeah, same really.'

'I start work early,' M. said, 'and it's a long day, and I
come home and I just want to cook and relax. I can't keep
going like this, you know?' He smiled shyly and looked at
me, almost embarrassed that he'd revealed too much.

'I can't keep *moving* like this,' I said, probably too quickly.
'Flat-hunting is a nightmare at the moment.'

He flicked the kettle on, and I wondered whether he'd
make me a cup of tea too.

'Well, it's open-ended, yeah? I've gotta see how I get on
with living with someone.'

'No, sure, yeah, no of course. I mean, I know your ad
said maybe only three months.'

The kettle began to hiss. I looked down, towards M.'s
feet again. His big toes filled out the front of his socks, but
there was no sign that his nails were long. Those chunky
big toes looked perfect, and I immediately tried to see his
hands. You can make a lot of educated guesses about some-
one's toes and feet from their hands, believe me. M. placed
his bum on a chair next to the kitchen table and lifted his
right foot, stacking the ankle atop his left knee.

'I have to wear boots on site, at work,' he said, as if he'd
seen me looking. He pressed his thumb pads into the ball
of his foot. 'I have to walk around and climb scaffolding all
day. It kills my feet.'

'Yeah,' I'd said. 'I... Erm.'

'Well, I've gotta make a start on this soup,' he said, tipping his head towards the beetroot. 'Lots to chop.'

'Sure. OK. I've got another viewing, so . . .'

He plonked his foot down onto the lino and pulled himself up. As the kettle clicked off, its steam spread between us. 'There's three more people coming to see the room tonight too,' he said. 'So let me know if you're interested.'

'Yep, I mean, yeah, sure, I'm definitely interested. It seems pretty chill.'

'Yeah, I am pretty chill,' he said. 'Cool, man. I'll text you.'

That's when I knew that my simple goal in life was to suck this man's toes.

*

I'm trying to plan it without planning it. Sometimes it feels like there is no way I can do this, but usually it also feels like something that I simply have to do. And I think M. needs it. I've watched him every day since I moved in. He falls onto the sofa in the evening like a sack of potatoes. He places his hands over his face and breathes heavily. When he speaks, he says that his supervising chief engineer doesn't understand all the things they have to do. He says they're over-budget, and the subcontractors make crazy demands. I know that M. has to convey all this to his seniors, so he's caught in the middle. He says that I don't need to know all this, and he's sorry for moaning. I say it's fine really.

When he eventually rises from the sofa to make himself some dinner, his shoulders are raised like those of a lioness, tense before pouncing on prey. But there's nothing for M.

to pounce on. His tension only releases a little when he unwinds at the kitchen worktop – chopping, frying, stirring, blending. I listen to his process, and sometimes watch the dance of his socked feet on the lino.

Sometimes I pretend to scratch my nose when I see him walk, just so that I can smell my fingertips. I'm always hoping there's enough of the scent of my own sweat that my brain might confuse it with what I see of his feet – that I might think my salty scent is his. Even at its weakest, it's stronger than the flavoured instant noodles in front of me.

M. gets up at 5.30 in the morning, showers, eats his bowl of overnight oats, and leaves by 6.00. It takes him forty-five minutes to get to the building site where he works. Everyone has to check in by 7.00 or they're docked pay and told not to come back tomorrow. They work until 5.00, which means I know he's always going to be home at 6.00. Fortunately, I'm done working by this point, and although I should be using the time to find somewhere more permanent to live, I choose to sit at the table so I can stare at his socks and suck my noodles.

Usually, he's on the sofa there for half an hour. Sometimes he even naps. Always he rises, then spends an hour in the kitchen. I've seen him ripping leaves onto meals, stirring spices into sauces he's nursing, and switching knives so he can slice the next vegetable exactly as he wants to. He usually eats in his bedroom.

It's a shame it's not summer right now. It's a shame the bathroom is right next to his bedroom, so I never catch a glimpse after his shower. I have to make-do with the steam he leaves behind, letting it coat my skin. It's a shame I can't just get down on the kitchen floor while he's cooking and touch his feet where his heels meet the lino, just there at the two concaves of his ankle leading down to the widening of the heel and the downward pressure onto the floor – all that looks perfect. And their smell must be mesmerising, at the end of the day, after being in his heavy boots for nearly twelve hours, in a physical job, sweating. They'll be red and swollen, and they'll need me to soothe them. That's what I'd do – rub them a little, releasing the smell up to my nostrils, then wash them, soak them, soap them, giving time to all the gaps between all the toes (which are not really gaps at all because they contain pleasures), and then dry them off, and rub them with chamomile oil, and rub and squeeze and press, noodling all the muscles and precious tendons. That's what I'd do. Something like that.

But I can't plan this. Licking toes is not usual behaviour, especially not from a flatmate without a contract. I need to stay in this place for a while. M. needs my money for the rent, and I haven't yet found anywhere with a permanent contract. I'm applying for ten flats every day and no one is getting back to me. Or they say the flat's gone already, within an hour of posting an ad. It's chaos out there. But M.'s place is all right. I've positioned the bed here in my room so that I can sit against the headboard to read in the pale sunlight in the morning.

*

M. hasn't come home from work tonight. I'm eating noodles again, slower and slower so there's still time for him to arrive and put his feet up. The flat is silent, and I have to watch TV just because it feels weird without M. there. When he finally arrives, I'm on the sofa watching a documentary about mushrooms. I shift quickly, folding my legs, so that he can join if he wants. He hesitates, then he hears the narrator say that fungi are genetically closer to humans than plants, and he says 'Woah', and finally sits down beside me. He smells like aftershave: some kind of fruity diesel. His heels rest on the floor, toes pointing up, and I'm probably staring at them because when the documentary ends he folds them underneath his body on the sofa. He says, 'Never dating again.'

'Oh . . . What happened?'

M. just shakes his head and inhales deeply – I feel these movements transfer to me through the sofa. I wonder if he'd relax enough to take his socks off.

'Ah, there's no point,' he says, unfolding himself to stand. 'Night.'

He disappears, and I hear him fill the kettle. I think about asking him to count me in for tea. For a second I consider turning down the TV sound and confessing that I, too, have given up on dating – in fact just before I moved in here. But I feel small, bunched up on the sofa, and I don't think he'd want to hear it. And anyway, he hasn't offered me a tea, so instead I just stare at an animated diagram of fungi spores.

Poor M. doesn't realise that tonight I could have relaxed him, soothed him, taken care of him, if only he'd given his feet over to me.

*

Tonight is the night. I'm in place at the table, trying to make sure that I have enough baked beans for every mouthful of toast. I usually grate cheese on top of this meal, but tonight I was deflated to see that I didn't have any cheese in the fridge. I am kicking myself about that when I hear the front door close. M. says hi, and I feel his body move the air around the flat as he walks across to the kitchen to pour a big glass of water. He gulps hard, exhales, then finally lays down on the sofa. The indentations on his socks are profound tonight – it's been a busy day. I can see the outlines of the toes, the balls, the heels, all perfect, and the thick cotton has been squished into his boots and will be unable to bounce back until washed.

'Beans on toast,' M. says, eyes closed, face turned towards the ceiling. 'Beans on toast for dinner?'

I freeze. My blood pressure rises. I feel it in my heartbeat. I'm confused, and, I think, a little hurt. It feels like an insult.

'Hey,' he says. 'Would you like me to cook a meal for you one night?'

He sits up, pulling his knees up, crossing his legs, his hands taking hold of his feet. His eyes are brighter than I've noticed before, as his face looks across at mine. 'If you want,' he shrugs, and even smiles.

'Ermmmm, sure,' I hear myself saying, above my heartbeat, ashamed and flushed at the same time. Then I say, 'Would you like me to clean and massage your feet for you?'

'Sounds good,' he says, falling backwards and relaxing again. 'Cool, man.'

*

So that's how it started. And this is how it's going. I'm kneeling on a thick towel on our living room floor, with my socks off. My erection is packed into my jeans, and there's a large bowl of steaming warm water between my legs. M. is on the sofa, and I'm removing his socks. He's shy, he tells me. He doesn't like the idea of showing his feet, he tells me. He's ticklish, he tells me. 'Relax,' I'm saying, over and over. 'Literally, M.: relax. Feel your muscles ease into the sofa. Let your head roll back, there, like that. Allow your chest to breathe openly, rise ... and fall ... rise ... and fall.'

I'm holding his right foot in my hand. I lean forward a little, so I can smell what I'm holding, and the scent is not strong but it is very, very, perfectly day-long sweaty. This is what he is scared of, but it is what I love. I begin to knead the soles of his feet, forcing my thumb into the ball of his foot. And this is when he moans. He must have heard himself, and been surprised, because he tenses up a little, but then decides this is too nice – I can feel him settle again, and I can hear him breathing.

'You like curry, right?' he says. 'I'll do a Chettinad chicken. I've been meaning to make one for ages.'

'OK, erm, sounds good.'

'Sweet. It's got lots of – ooo, that's nice – lots of toasted spices, and coconut.'

I begin to bathe his right foot, and I'm already anticipating the left one. It's resting right there, fresh, beside my knee, waiting for the dry rub first. The water roils around M.'s foot in the bowl, as my hands continue their work. M. moans again. My fingers push through, between his toes. I use the flannel I brought in from the bathroom, to make sure the soap in the water is wiping away everything it can from his precious skin.

'I like coconut curries,' I say, thinking that the creamy water I'm using isn't too far from coconut milk.

'What about cardamom?'

I say I don't know that, and he says it's a spice, more of a flavour. He says he'll use them in the curry he'll make. He says, 'You need something better than instant noodles and beans on toast.'

I've stopped. My hands float in the water, above his foot. I've stopped because suddenly I'm thinking about M. making a meal for me. M. wants to cook a curry and give some to me.

'I like it from the takeaway when they' – I'm talking fast and I can barely get the words out in the right order – 'when they put the crispy onions on top.'

'I can do that,' he says, lifting his left foot up for me. 'Shallots are best for that. In butter, for more than half an hour. Really slow.'

I give his left big toe a kiss, and then I begin to work on it, as his right one sits drying on my thigh. I'm thinking of the extremely rapid wank I'll have to do very soon.

*

The next night M. carries two bowls of thick red curry to the table. I look down at the meal in front of me: it is rich, the colour of lava, with flicks of green and black from various spices in the sauce. Shards of brown, crisped shallots are piled on top. I inhale the deep aromas as he returns to the worktop to fetch another bowl – steaming white rice this time. It smells like hot purity.

When M. sits down across from me, he places his socked foot on top of mine, on the thin carpet. And we smile like boys because something here is silly, but it's silly for both of us.

'You know what,' he says, 'when you next need a really big piss, would you tell me? I'll get in the bathtub and you can stand over me and let it all go. Would you do that for me?'

Adam Zmith (he/him) is always working on a novel. He is the author of *Deep Sniff: A History of Poppers and Queer Futures* (Repeater Books, 2021). He is also the writer and producer of the BBC podcast series *The Film We Can't See*, a co-producer of *The Log Books* podcast, and co-director of the podcast production company Aunt Nell.

I Attempt to Explain My Sexuality at a Kink Event While Slowly Realising I Want You – Emilija Ducks

I say noetisexual but it's not quite right it can take a while
I'd say demisexual but it's not quite right it might take a
couple of hours **have you by any chance had your child-
hood riddled with trauma** cos you sure as fuck don't look
twenty-one and that's what I was told at your age my ex is
triggering across the room got hooked on his NRE his here
and then disappear made wet my disorganised attachment
he'd clumsily cast a net I tucked myself in now he looks
mousy and plain like unbuttered bread and you intimidate
still I do the butterfly technique in the bathroom the tiles
go from blurry to clear and at the end of the night you calm
volunteer I say **if you'll tolerate my incompetence** your
movements form a solid yes good god deep breaths   hit it:
    I've never been better with the whip and paddle
       leave marks with the firehose attached to a handle
    I've done quite a few but this fucking feels right

lashes on your strong back, mist of sweat, your head
is down
I worship you mutely and touch every sore spot
you say I'm the best one to do it on this night.

you
have

a

black
line
tattoo
along
your
spine

well fuck.

Emilija Ducks (they/them), born in Macedonia, is a non-binary musician and writer, active in both fields since their adolescence. They are self-taught in poetry and musically educated. Published in Macedonia, Serbia and England, they have released two EPs and a single which are available on Spotify and other listening platforms. Emilija is currently based in Manchester and probably doing chainmail or something.

The End of the Friend –
Karen McLeod

It's two thirty in the morning, and the final night I will think of Angela as my friend. We don't know anything about this yet. How could we? We are doing what we always do: we meet in The Hope and Anchor to discuss Angela's marriage and get drunker than is sane. Every betrayal, each tiny violence unfolds from her mouth as a slap on top of the next glorious confidence. Of course, *he's* at home with the bottle, so we drink until closing time, then order a mini cab back to my flat. On the way, we stop at the late-night wine shop with its shutters half down and shout through the gap for crisps and half-decent wine. We feel lucky if they serve us, as if we're winning at life.

'Days are constructs,' Angela says, finishing her glass.

We know so much of each other, we can say things like this without thinking it pretentious. I fill her glass straight away, forever the hostess. Up until now my house has been a world of perpetual drinking, where if the glass is not full, someone is either asleep or ill.

The morning out the window looks like it won't come and there's a freedom to this part of the night. Angela goes round and round again about her marriage, and I let her do it, because it fills me up. I get to borrow Angela's marriage as if it were mine, and her problems become my problems. But more than this, I enjoy the ruin of it all. For now, these troubles are the only ones in the world, and we thoroughly intend to excavate them.

There will be nothing much left of us by the end of the night. This is the part I enjoy, the eradicating of myself. But it's the very thing I should guard against. I should've learned to watch out for this by now, this emptying of rooms.

'Let's play some other music,' Angela says.

'Christine is asleep though,' I say, nodding at the lounge door. 'I'd rather . . .'

'She can't begrudge music; it's Saturday night,' she says.

'I thought days were constructs?'

'Only weekdays.'

In this instant all I can do is stare at Angela's ear and think what a weird-shaped entrance it is for a person's head. I try not to focus on the grey clip behind the lobe, the angle of it, as it makes me feel too much for her. The door to the hall is shut; Christine must be sleeping. She didn't even appear in the bedroom doorway when we came in.

'What you thinking?' Angela says.

'Nothing much,' I say, pressing myself into the sofa cushions. But I am lying, as I do know what I'm think-ing, which is how I shouldn't turn up the music because Christine is in bed. Our relationship is young, fragile, so it could be snuffed out effortlessly. Our living together is novel. We are giving it a go.

'That a new painting?' Angela says, pointing at the large canvas over the record player.

'It is,' I say. 'One of Christine's.'

'Oh,' Angela says. She rubs her nose, then examines her finger.

'I like the green shadows over the monkey's face,' I say.

'Well,' Angela says. 'It's different to what you would usually have up.'

In the corner of the painting are Christine's initials, CC, faintly scratched in red. The music is on quietly – an early album from Penguin Cafe Orchestra. I will not turn it up; I like to think this particular volume creates the perfect ambience.

I fell in love with Angela on the top bunk of a youth hostel in Berlin. We were on an art college trip. People didn't belong as absolutely to other people back then. The barriers, which in adult life seem so solid and fixed, did not exist for us at art school.

I'd been out, discovering Berlin by bar hopping and found a tiny lesbian club where, to my delight, the butch manager said no men were permitted. In the corner a drag queen sat alone on a banquette, singing morose German songs into a microphone.

As a storm buffered the windows back at the hostel, I ran my finger over Angela's stomach, the skin vibrating underneath the tip. My dungarees had twisted up uncomfortably with all the writhing, so I'd taken them off. We were naked, kissing on the top bunk, but l didn't want to go further as this would make me into a full-time lesbian. I didn't get to find out what would happen next because the window of the dorm flung itself open, crashing the wooden frame against the wall. The glass didn't break, but the bitter wind made enough of an entrance to make me believe Angela's boyfriend had declared himself.

The next morning, over breakfast, Angela held up a soft-boiled egg and said this was what I was. Just an egg; a baby.

'You see,' Angela says. 'Marriage is a good thing, if you want to be left alone.' She stretches her arm along the back of the sofa, so it brushes my shoulder. I feel the familiar long-ago thrill, more like a memory of the thrill, alongside a present discomfort.

'Last night he had his hands around your neck,' I remind her.

Angela grasps her wine glass and the wine rocks from side to side. She drinks it down automatically. 'So?' she says. 'He never meant it. He was drunk.' I refill the glass, but there is something about Angela that I am afraid of now.

'What about his upbringing?' I say. Amateur psychologist. 'What kind of people were his parents?' I cannot know I asked this same question an hour before.

'Perfectly nice people, a bit pedestrian if anything,' Angela says.

'Oh well, some people have to be,' I say. 'Dull, I mean. So others aren't. Like us.'

'Yes, like us,' she says, snuggling down and giving me that smile.

We are onto the third bottle. Angela shakes it to find an inch at the bottom. It'll soon be time to rummage in the cupboard.

'You know, things could've been so different,' she says sighing. 'If only you'd been more confident back then.'

'I know,' I say.

Last night Angela woke to her husband on top of her, his hands shaking her awake. Before this he'd fallen in the garden, bloodied his nose, wet his trousers.

'Angela, do you ever worry maybe we could be alcoholics?'

'No,' she says.

'But how do you know?'

'Because my husband is one.'

Kneeling by the record player, Angela studies the albums. Her thighs are trim, no fat at all. Her blonde hair is plaited in two so I can see a line of scalp running down the back of her head. Pulling out a record, she tilts the cover to face me, and I shrug, yes. It's Morrissey's *Viva Hate*. She drops the needle on the right spot, 'Every Day Is Like Sunday'. Then I watch her turn up the volume. I don't want it that loud, but, aren't we still young? Shouldn't we defy convention and the notion of being good?

I relent. Let it play on, after all, isn't there enough sadness in Angela's life to allow her just the one song, a bit loud, on a Saturday night? In the morning I will explain all this to Christine, how because of the circumstances, the music had to be turned up. Besides, this is the meaning of being a best friend, to be there for the pain and then try to house it.

Morrissey goes on for some time, then Angela puts on a series of seven-inch records. Out the window in the distance a police car crawls up the hill, the blue lights reflecting off the houses.

It is between songs, I hear the toilet flush. Then the door to our bedroom shuts as firmly as possible although the carpet gets in the way. I don't say anything, I just walk over to the record player and turn the music down. Angela watches, I feel her, even with my back turned.

'Bit too much,' I say.

'Really?'

This is my flat, I want to spell out. I want to say how the sound in the block travels at night and my neighbour has banged on the kitchen wall in the past. But all this makes me seem too adult, too conventional. I don't go and check on Christine although I want to. As long as the lounge door stays shut the two worlds remain separate. But who am I kidding? It is more complex than I am able to think about right now, so I go to the kitchen and open the bottles cupboard. Behind the sunflower oil is the supermarket brandy for the peppercorn sauce. The one I made to woo Christine on the night I asked her to move in.

'Lovely,' Angela says, lighting a cigarette. She inhales deeply, then sips the brandy. I take a drag and enjoy the smoke hitting my lungs. Christine has given up as she suffers with asthma, but everyone knows smoking is about freedom.

Angela and I are now either end of the new charcoal-grey sofa from Habitat. It is the most expensive piece of major furniture I have ever had. Christine bought it with her redundancy money. Nine hundred pounds, it folds out into a double bed with its own mattress. Me and Christine sat on it in the showroom and said, yes, this feels like it could be us.

The next morning Christine is not beside me when I wake in our bed. I vaguely recall getting in, lifting the duvet and finding Christine not moving in that rigid way which implies more than is said.

When I can face it, I enter the lounge and find Angela on the couch under a blanket. We sit drinking tea, nursing the away feeling in my body as I am still full of alcohol. Two hours pass easily, and Angela doesn't make a move to go home, and I don't want to ask her to leave. I believe we are OK, that nothing is changed. That nothing needs to.

Still I attend to Angela, and it is only when she is in the bath I feel space enough to check my phone. There is no message from Christine, and I wonder where she could be on a Sunday. I tidy the lounge, even take out the polish to make the room smell unburdened. It is then I notice a mark on the sofa. On closer inspection I find a hole, a burn mark, where the white foam shines from beneath. It's in the centre of the cushion, a place which can't be hidden by a throw, or scatter cushion. Pulling the cushion up, I discover Velcro holds it in place underneath and my ears go hot.

With black cotton, and one eye on the door in case Angela appears, I stitch it over and over, trying to thatch it into something which might go unnoticed. As I am doing it I wonder whether I could pretend nothing has happened. Then when I am done sewing, I try to flatten the thread so it will lay plush with the cushion cover.

Noticing the record player is still on, I turn it off at the plug, then stare up at Christine's artwork. The painting is not as well executed as I had first believed; the monkey's eyes are crossed. The colours more burnt wood than green.

Loudly hoovering outside the bathroom, I tell myself Angela is not to blame, it is me who didn't tell her not to smoke. When Angela finally exits the bathroom, damp and squeaky-faced, wrapped in a towel, she says, 'morning' in a fresh note as if the night is behind her. I make peanut butter on toast, and we sit talking about the missed calls on her phone. Even though she is beside the hole on the sofa, she has not noticed. I ask if she is going back to him tonight? She says she doesn't know. Could she perhaps hang out here, until it's time to go for her shift later?

I am lifted by the realisation she will, at some point, be gone for work at the nightclub. I make an excuse of needing to go to Sainsburys, so I suggest I could walk her to the bus station at the same time? She should surely go home to get her nightclub clothes. Before we leave, we stand in the lounge, finding more to talk about, and the hole is so obvious.

Just before we leave, she pats her pockets for her house keys. In the lounge she searches down the side of the sofa and I am sure this is when she notices, as there is a thought running over her face, like a cloud over the sun. But still, as we walk down the high street, away from the flat, we link arms like we always do, and neither of us says a thing. I hope the chill winter air will strip the puffiness away from my face and return the day to normal.

'See you soon,' I say, at the bus stop.

'I'll need a bit more space from him I think,' she says. 'Can I stay over tonight?'

'Oh,' I say. 'Why don't you text me later?'

The pull between her and me is impossible.

'Right,' she says. 'I can stay, can't I?'

'Of course,' I say. 'Call me later.'

Even though I know the heart is a renewable thing, that every cell dies and is replaced with a new one, it's the scar, the badly sewn hole which waits for me at home. Once back, I make the flat so neat there can be no other fault found. Angela has left her socks on the bathroom floor, so

I throw them in the kitchen bin, wondering whether she's bare foot in her trainers.

Then I sit on the sofa-hole, hoping it'll flatten and mend itself while I wait for Christine. Studying the painting, I scrutinise the monkey's face. Isn't it out of proportion, the mouth a little too human? Do monkeys have philtrums? I press my eyes, then open them swiftly to examine it afresh. But I cannot see the painting in the same pure light I once had. Angela has contaminated it.

When I hear the door click open, and the jangling of keys as they hit the bowl, I sit up straight, then lean to one side so it's like I am casually thinking. Christine will be taking off her shoes and I hold my breath, my heart pounding, and wait for the tread of her feet along the corridor. I brighten my face by stretching open my mouth, then closing it. Before she reaches me, my phone is vibrating.

Angela.

I switch it to silent, before placing it behind my back. I cannot bring myself to turn it completely off, as that would be all too cruel.

———

Karen McLeod is a published author and established writer and performer. Her debut novel, *In Search of the Missing Eyelash*, was published by Jonathan Cape, won the Betty Trask Award, was shortlisted for the Best First Novel Award and translated into four languages. Writer-in-residence at Bookseller Crow on the Hill, Karen performs as the celebrated comic poet character Barbara Brownskirt. Her memoir, *Lifting Off*, will be published by Muswell Press in 2024.

Farewell to a Model – Jerl Surratt

You're tired of me and done with this, my trying
to build you up by showing you how strong
you look as a saint in the Academic style,
talking you up with such passion while painting
in hope you'd find in being depicted
as someone worthy of adoration
a refuge from your drinking and your dope.

Now in the wake of being lightly robbed
and rebuked again, sketching from memory
a few more late-night portraits of you
you wouldn't think much of, and I'll rip up
tomorrow, I blame myself for pretending to
a kindness that intended less to enchant
than to protect you, as though with my own hands

I might suppress forces I presumed to argue
with you could kill you. Rightly you weren't
persuaded I meant by this I cared about just you.
I've seen too many young men die unhaloed,
everyone left behind in some part guilty

of failing to convince them of their beauty,
and each one, like the first one, one too many.

But what am I doing, drawing this to a close?
It's you that I adore. Why have I turned into
the kind of scold that you grew up against –
the father figure who withheld his love
for never being in control of you, who made
a co-dependent man of you, then set you free.
Come back, is all I want to say right now,

and come of age again before my eyes.
And maybe in a night or two, the way it's been,
you will. And what I'll try to tell you then,
if so, is that I've feared to feel till now
another love that's unconditional
for someone younger I might well outlive
and why you are too beautiful for words.

––––––––––––––––––––

Jerl Surratt was born in rural Texas and educated by New York City, where he helped raise funds for PWA/LGBTQ+ civil rights organisations and other progressive groups. His poems have been published in *The Hopkins Review, Kenyon Review, Literary Imagination, The New Criterion* and elsewhere. In 2020, he was awarded the Tor House Prize for Poetry by judge Marie Howe. www.jerlsurratt.com

The Artist is Present – Sarah Keenan

As we head north on the M25, I begin to realise that we are
going on holiday with Marina Abramović. You went to see
her exhibition at the Tate yesterday, your weekly 'artist date'
with yourself. I encouraged you to take these dates after the
final surgery, when you were learning to live with your leg,
and eight years later you keep up the practice. Today Marina
Abramović is all you can speak about.

You lean back in the passenger seat and cradle your phone
in front of your face like a new pet hamster. As I navigate
our way around consecutive HGVs, our Citroën merging
into the dirty stream of metal and rubber, you tell me about
the cutting-edge, bold embodiment of her performances,
how in her early work she had cut her own hand with a
knife, let audience members stick rose thorns into her stom-
ach, and more than once had become unconscious from
intentionally breathing in too much air or inhaling smoke
from a fire she had lit and then thrown herself into.

'She sets up the mutilation of her body as a public event,
so her body becomes an object, but one that she owns and
can do whatever she wants with.' You pause, look out at
the blue Ford Fiesta in front of us. It is a mild August day,

and you keep your window slightly open even though I am driving at 70 miles per hour and the rush of air into the car means you have to speak at an amplified volume.

Marina Abramović's work has become less physically risky as she has grown older, you explain, but it is still just as emotionally powerful. You describe a recent performance in which she stared at her ex-lover across a table, crying silently, then taking his hands in hers as the audience erupted in applause.

'They'd had a really dramatic breakup and not spoken for years.' You set your phone down in your lap. 'And then she was doing this performance at MOMA where she would look people in the eye as they sat across from her − total strangers you know, just members of the public − really look right at them for a minute or so, to see what emotions that connection brought into the room. She'd sit there for hours, closing her eyes as one person left and opening them once the next had arrived. Then she opened her eyes and there he was! She had no idea he was coming.' You are almost breathless with excitement.

'Sounds intense,' I offer.

'We should watch it on YouTube later,' you say, retrieving your phone. You search for podcasts about the history of performance art and continue to educate me about Marina Abramović's career.

When I wake on the first morning of our holiday, you're gone. We are at an Airbnb which you found, so I have been pretending not to share your horror at the relentless butterfly decor and proximity of the 'cottage' to the owners' house. Perhaps you have made good on your threat to complain to the owners about being able to hear their bathroom noises through our bedroom wall. Perhaps you are making us breakfast.

I climb out of bed and find you at the living room table with your laptop open, writing an essay about Marina Abramović. It is a grey day in Northumberland, and the view from the butterfly cottage is not the 'five star, breath-taking vista' the reviews suggested. I make us breakfast.

'Shall we go out for a big walk today?' I ask. As I near the end of my scrambled eggs, the image of a large multi-coloured butterfly materialises on the plate beneath.

'Well I don't want to stay in this place all day,' you answer.

We pack some snacks, fill our water bottles, and close the butterfly-motif gate behind us as we head out to find the walking paths. Friends of friends had told us about stunning hikes through open heather moors, colourful dales and lush meadows in this area, but we spend the day walking 21 kilometres through endless fields most notable for their barking dogs and disused tractors. There is absolutely no one else around, even the farmers seem to have fled, and each time I hear a car I feel a rush of both relief and fear. After the first hour you realise I have reached my limit on Marina Abramović, and we walk in silence. I stay behind you out of habit, and occasionally notice the strange perfection of your gait.

The pathways are poorly marked: we have to go back on ourselves, and after four hours we run out of food. We manage to navigate to a coal mining museum, where thankfully the cafe is open. But by the time we make it back to the cottage, you are angry with boredom and fatigue. I feel fairly numb. We watch an episode of Ru Paul's Drag Race and go to bed early.

*

Back in the car, I drive us further north towards Oban. We stop in Glasgow for lunch, where you want to go to all the independent bookstores in the area and look at their art selections. In one I find a jigsaw of a vintage Chinese cigarette ad, featuring the cartoonish image of two women in colourful cheongsams, smiling by a piano in a dimly lit saloon. I point it out to you. We had loved looking through these kinds of posters in the antique stores in Shanghai when we went to visit your family years ago. We would rummage through to find the ones with pairs of women selling luxury consumer products in 1920s China: tobacco, wine, radios, insect repellent. There is still a framed one hanging in our living room at home, for Tsingtao beer. You smile, *oh cool*, but the puzzle doesn't make it into the armful of printed material you take to the cashier. I rescue the puzzle from its shelf and line up behind you. Engrossed in one of the books you're about to purchase, you don't notice me until you turn to exit the store.

'Oh, I thought you'd gone outside to wait,' you say, looking down at the shiny box in my hands. 'Sorry I didn't realise you wanted it. I could have bought it with my books . . .'

'It's fine,' I interrupt. 'I just thought maybe it'd be nice to do at the cottage.'

'Yes!' you reply, emphatic, 'really good idea.'

We walk back to the car without speaking.

Our Scottish cottage is filled with empty shelves and plastic plants, but it is properly ours for the week: fully detached with no 'hosts' in sight, access being via the infinitely preferable key lock box. It also has big bay windows with a view out to the cold, grey sea and the mountains behind it. Perhaps we will have a nice time together here.

But your main desire is still to be with your laptop, and you have also become adept at writing on your phone. Every minute you catch alone – when I am working out how to use the DVD player, when I leave the room to pee, when we're out and I go to the counter to order us lunch – you grab your phone and keep writing your essay. Sometimes you pretend to be texting, but you focus on the small screen with such intensity, I know you are with Marina in your mind. That evening you spend so long in the bedroom 'putting another layer on' after dinner that our ice cream starts to melt while I wait to restart the film. You say that you were looking for your woollen jumper, but I notice when you finally return that you had your phone with you the whole time.

I set up the jigsaw on the table by the bay windows, making sure to leave just enough space for laptops and meals. You work on the jigsaw straight after breakfast. Impatient with the process, I worry you are damaging the pieces by forcing them into incorrect alignments. After about an hour of jigsaw labour you return to your laptop. For the rest of these days we sit at the table, me gently fingering the puzzle's coloured cardboard fragments, you typing with great ferocity, rarely looking up.

On day four I drive us to Loch Lomond. A day trip. It starts out well. Neither of us has been here before, and both our moods brighten as we look around at the snow-capped mountains and unending expanse of fresh water. The sky is wider here, more feels possible. Staring out at the loch, we briefly hold hands. There are no walking paths, so we decide to splurge on kayaks. I eye the doubles and feel excited to be close to you for an hour, away from all your screens.

'We'll get singles yeah?' You say, studying the blackboard of prices.

'Yeah cool, great.'

From the moment we hit the water you are faster than me. I find this strange because I am usually stronger than you, but I am paddling as hard as I can and you are disappearing into the windy waters ahead.

'You decide where next,' you slow down and holler back to me as we arrive at the first rocky island.

'Um ...' I prevaricate, trying to pre-empt what you want. I want to potter around, not go any further.

'Let's just do a drive-by over here,' you shout, paddling towards another island.

'A what?'

'Just paddle by, to look at the wildlife, not that we'll probably see any.' You are beaming.

'OK,' I say, but you do not hear me. You are already too far ahead.

Along the first stretch of this small island it is peaceful. Still water, lush green yew trees growing out of rocks, mountains behind us and not another kayaker in sight. My arms are tired, and you stay so far ahead it's impossible to talk to you about the beauty we are witnessing, but I am still enjoying myself. As we come to round the bend another island appears behind this one. We turn to paddle through the water between them, but that water quickly runs into rock: the second island is actually a continuation of the first, which is much bigger than we thought. Should we turn back rather than try to go all the way around? We don't know how far this island extends. I want to share my worries with you but you keep paddling further and further into the distance. I follow you, defeated, noticing the darkness of the water. As we round another bend the wind changes. The waves beneath us become more aggressive, tussling our small plastic boats from below. My whole upper body aches and I am out of breath. The green life on the island has turned to a long patch of smooth black rock. The shore of our departure has completely disappeared from view.

Occasionally you glance back. I shout your name, 'I'm scared!' but you have already turned back again, you cannot hear me. As we round another bend, the extent of our distance from shore becomes evident. I start to cry, still paddling, breathing hard. Bursts of rage bubble up in between my rising panic, which at least helps spur me on.

Eventually you notice me. You slow down, shocked, and wait for me to catch up. The waves continue to rock our kayaks, now causing me a mild nausea. You seem agitated at my distress.

'What's wrong!?' It's an accusation.

I explain that I've been shouting at you for a long time but you didn't hear.

'Do you want me to do the emergency signal?' you ask.

At our safety briefing, back on the shore a lifetime ago, a young man with a navy jumper and a thick Scottish accent told us that if we were in trouble we should hold our oars vertically in the air, as a kind of flagless pole, if we needed to call for help. But there is no way they will spot us out here. We have to keep paddling.

'Sorry,' you apologise as we propel ourselves forward. Still crying, I cannot look at you.

*

The day they told you that you had to have surgery, you insisted we walk the long way home, through Piccadilly Arcade.

'Because if they fuck up my surgery I might never walk again.'

I told you to stop being ridiculous.

We stopped at the overpriced deli, where I bought you a tin of chocolates, bright red and shaped like a heart. When I presented it to you, you smiled but pushed it back to me, 'these are for when I'm better.' When we finally peeled off the plastic seal around the lid more than two years later, the truffles had gone dry. I made up a story about having just rediscovered them at the back of the cupboard, so as not to upset you, but you seemed unburdened by the tin's history. 'Yum,' you said, studying its expired contents, 'I'm sure they're still OK to eat.'

The morning we checked in at the hospital for the main event, I brought Assata Shakur's autobiography for us to read in the waiting room, which was not a good choice. No one wants to read about police violence while they're waiting to be cut open by strangers, not even you. And now we'll never know the full details of her amazing escape from prison and life on the run in Cuba. Now we'll never know about that.

As we sat on the faded blue plastic chairs, memorising the pattern of the linoleum flooring beneath us, I distracted myself from what was about to happen to you by investing in the drama of everyone's operations. I watched each party – no one was there alone – wondering who was the patient, and what they were having done. Surely as part of this vibrant squad of West London's injured and ailing, all of them loved and cared for, surely you would be OK. You can trust doctors, I kept telling you, this is one of the best health systems in the world. You always worry too much. It will be over soon. Try to relax.

When your name was first called by a clean-cut, white-coated young man looking down at a clipboard, I sat bolt upright, almost high on adrenalin. But it was just a pre-surgery consultation. You walked alone through the double doors – 'Patients Only' – and I only noticed later that all the straight couples ignored the sign and went in and out of those consultations together. It was almost three in the afternoon when a kindly young woman in a blue nurse's uniform finally called you for real. We had been there since 7 a.m. I hugged you goodbye, *see you in like three hours*. I hoped the surgeons weren't tired. I hoped they understood who you were, not just an Asian female body on a silver tray, but a small miracle who was a whole woman, who laughed and cried and ate and made the most hilarious hand puppets out of aeroplane socks and volunteered at the local soup kitchen most Sundays but only in secret lest your friends think you earnest.

I took the elevator to the ground floor for a change of scene. They had Portuguese custard tarts at the cafe so I bought one for you, for after. Because you love those. I found a free seat across from a table of young doctors drinking coffee from Costa cups, and looked down at my phone. You had texted seven minutes ago, just after I left you. I unlocked my screen in a panic.

[14.59 You:
I'm in another waiting room with one other person. Don't like how young all the doctors look.]

I texted back immediately.

[15.06 Me:
So sorry I just saw this. Came downstairs for air.]

[15.06 Me:
The doctors know what they're doing and will take care of you.]

[15.06 Me:
You're going to be completely fine, I promise.]

[15.06 Me:
I love you.]

I glared at my screen willing you to reply. Was I too late? My heart raced, I became tearful. They had probably taken you to theatre by now. You were relying on me and I had abandoned you. I looked over at the Costa-drinking junior doctors in desperation. My face felt flushed and for some reason I wanted to call your mother. Then three dots appeared in a small blue box.

[15.07 You:
OK Brewster, I'll try to be brave. They're going to put my things in a locker now. I love you too.]

Brewster was your pet name for me, based on a TV show I loved as a child, about an orphan girl and her dog making do in downtown Chicago. I exhaled, looked around the cafe again. She's all right! I shouted in my head at the table of doctors and the various strangers walking by. You were going to be all right.

To help pass the time I pulled out my headphones and put on a podcast about a group of women of colour in Bristol who squatted an abandoned building and were using it as a headquarters for their campaign to pay reparations to local survivors of colonialism by requisitioning all corporate bonuses paid in the city last year. How about that? I couldn't wait to talk to you about it.

*

As we approach the shore, the silhouette of the kayak hire hut sharpens, and fluorescently clothed tourists in chunky hiking boots come into view. We are going to survive. You land a few minutes before me, pull your boat onto the sand and hurry over to speak to navy jumper man. We only hired these kayaks for an hour and I am positive we have been on the water for at least five.

'We were out for about an hour and a half but he says it's OK,' you say as I step, jelly-legged, onto the sand. You reach your arm out to steady me. I accept it, but need to be free of you. I march to the car in silence, conscious of people looking at us.

The next morning you wake early.

'I want to go for a swim,' you announce from the hall-way, already up and dressed. I pull the covers higher.

You like cold water swimming. You are always pushing your body, punishing it, trying to make it stronger. Even since before.

I should let you go alone, but I walk down and watch you from the beach. It's deserted, aside from a man in a woollen coat and hat who walks by with his black Labrador, throwing a tennis ball for the dog with one of those long plastic launchers. You thrash through the waves, striking back at the cold as it envelops your body, swimming madly at first and then with a calmer stroke as you adjust. When you resurface onto land, shivering and triumphant, I cannot believe how beautiful you are.

'I finished my essay yesterday,' you tell me as I wrap you in a towel, 'so you can stop being so upset with me all the time.'

I hand you your prosthetic and you pull it on like a sock. It's top of the range, carbon–fibre, flexible, comfortable. They said it should last about twenty-five years, so we hope you'll need three of them.

'After we got back?' I ask as you pull on your thick fleece hoodie, 'when did you manage that?'

You shrug. 'I had almost finished it.'

We walk up the sandbank and to the empty beach car park. You are walking briskly now. I hurry along beside you, trying to keep up. An older woman in an expensive beach dressing robe steps out of her car. She sees you, wet and jittery, and gives you an enormous smile. You exchange greetings as we rush along the footpath.

After breakfast we sit together before the jigsaw, letting its pieces spill out over the full surface of the table. It is about one third complete. I have been concentrating on the outline, which looks up at us, an expectant white frame. In the space inside it, the bulk of the women's cheongsams hover like moth-eaten headless models. We spend hours switching our gaze between individual pieces and the emerging picture, pulled into the drama of the black lines, soft curves and quietly clashing tones of the image.

'So Marina Abramović, I'm not completely on board with everything she's done,' you say as you scan through pieces of differently shaded white. 'I mean bodies *are* complicated and interesting –' you draw back in a moment of satisfaction as the piece of face you have been handling finally slots into place, '– but maybe sometimes artists are searching for meaning and connection where there isn't any, you know?'

I pause to look up at you, meeting your deep green eyes. 'Not really.'

We return to the jigsaw, willing the complete picture to appear.

———————————

Sarah Keenan is a London-based writer and teacher originally from Giabal and Jarowair land in Toowoomba, 'Australia'.

Queens Road Peckham –
JP Seabright

The morning after my fortieth birthday I stood on the station platform after staying the night at my friend's. Since daybreak I'd been on his laptop sending messages to you on Faccbook to ask where you were where had you been why did you not come and meet me and sorry if you called and I didn't reply but my phone had been nicked just hours before in the RVT by a man who was dancing close to me which felt kinda sexy in the nightclub sweat and alcoholic haze of my birthday cocktails but proved only stupid when I discovered it gone pinched like my arse by a stranger in the dark. I stood on the platform that Aquarian morning a new decade before me and recalled your reply how you went somewhere else couldn't be bothered to meet which was fine on one level as we weren't an item not even a label just an occasional shag (not a great one at that) and I wasn't that fussy but it was my birthday and it was customary to get laid so I'll be honest I was disappointed I'd expected more not just a grope and kiss under the Vauxhall arches but we never spoke again after that.

Maybe 'cause I wrote to you just a few days later once I had a replacement phone to tell you that I'd stood on the station platform that post-birthday morning and it was all I could do not to throw myself screaming onto the tracks and into the path of the oncoming train.

High & Dry — JP Seabright

...the time in that pub in Old Compton Street, my first time in gay Soho with a girlfriend, we were there for Pride I think, I don't know, I can't remember, but I remember this: standing, my back against the wall, arse impaled on the radiator to maintain my position, a slot machine nearby to my left, or was it a cigarette machine, possibly both, these were gambling and smoking days, under my feet, dirty brown sticky floorboards, worn with the hope and fears of a thousand queers, drinking, dancing, laughing, flirting, snogging in the bogs and fucking round the back, a quickie in the cut-through to Rupert Street, but not us, not that time, I just stood there *wishing we could still make love*, we were in the Duke of Wellington, not the one I would later come to frequent with my next girlfriend, the one after you, our local in Dalston, one of the last places I saw my uncle alive, its closure now made even more poignant, end of an era and all that, but the one 300 feet and four years away from a bombed-out Admiral Duncan, walls and arms and heads studded with neo-Nazi nails, and I stood there watching everyone around me drinking and dancing and laughing and flirting, and I looked at you, yes you BillySue, looking at your friend, joking and messing about, *thinking you've got the world all sussed out*, whilst I was trying to work out how to appear normal, now that I knew what normal should look like for a baby dyke, yet merely *drying up in conversation* with your other friend, who was nice but a little insipid and he didn't know if he was gay or not yet, was just along for the ride, and I looked at you looking at your friend and I knew then that it was over and this song started playing by Radiohead and I was swallowed by this song, entirely whole, I disappeared inside it, it enveloped me, it knew me intimately, it was singing the emotional mess inside my head and the ache in my body, don't leave me, high, or dry, but you did, not then, not even that month, but the next one, when you had the guts to tell me, but only after I'd gone down on you without any reciprocation, and at the time I thought that this was *the best thing that I'll ever have,* the best thing that I nearly had, 'cos for a short while I had you, and we were the talk of the town, the bees knees, you were top dog and I was your bitch, for a while, but then it wasn't the best thing was it, not even close, just one of the first things, and now you're a drag king performing karaoke in a grimy tourist bar in Marbella or Magaluf or somewhere like that and I haven't seen you now for over twenty-five years but sometimes I think of you and that exact moment whenever I hear that song and I hope you're happy now . . .

JP Seabright (she/they) is a queer disabled writer living in London. They have three pamphlets published: *Fragments from Before the Fall: An Anthology in Post-Anthropocene Poetry* (Beir Bua Press, 2021), *No Holds Barred* (Lupercalia Press,

2022), and *GenderFux* (Nine Pens Press, 2022). *Machinations*, a collaborative experimental work, was published in 2022. More info at jpseabright.com and via Twitter @ errormessage.

A Character Sketch – Gaar Adams

He considered the request while standing on his tiptoes, just tall enough to rest his dick over the lip of the sink.

May I sketch you?

The tap always ran cold. He winced, bracing the chipped enamel of the basin with one hand, pulling back his foreskin and washing with the other. It was certainly unusual. Then again, perhaps the whole deluge of requests he'd fielded in the years since his arrival could be classified as unusual, too: the erotic tickling, the genital electrostimulation, the invitation to watch a man wank in the rugby kit of his ex-lover during the half-time of a Sevens match. But life modelling? The idea enticed him: that he might be regarded, if only for an hour, as a paragon of anything.

He checked the man's address, swishing a flake of crusted toothpaste and a mouthful of water into a frothy lather. Four miles. Even without the rain, it was further than he would have liked. But the tidiness in the man's rapid-fire messages charmed him, a stark contrast to the three-word fragments and grunted voice notes he usually received. The man had ended each one with such thoughtful punctuation. *I can show it to you when I'm finished if you'd like?* He spat an ellipsis of successive little globules and watched it recede towards the drain like seafoam at low tide. The mirror, speckled with a film of toothpaste and grime, had needed a clean for some time now. Banging out a quick response with his thumbs – *b there in 45* – he left the question and the task, a devil emoji his only punctuation mark.

A shadow leaning against the open door of the first house on the man's street nodded to him. He rifled in his pocket to fish out his phone, the city's address system still periodically confounding him, but the figure waved him up the steps. He felt a decisiveness at the core of the man's movements that pulled him across the unlit threshold and assured him that he had arrived in the right place.

In the corner of the man's dim foyer, he folded his wet coat and socks and placed them atop his shoes. He'd come to recognise the value of a careful undressing in these situations. Best to leave his soaking outer layers by the door and keep his undergarments in a neat pile within reach of the nightstand, stripping once the lamp had been switched off. Searching for the errant undershirt or boxers, he'd found that it was all too easy to get lost in the murk of a place that was not his. Still, he allowed the man to pick up his damp clothes, watching the front window fog as he draped each article over his radiator.

The man ushered him into the living room and flicked on a torchiere. It cast a dim glow but offered just enough to get a clear view of this stranger. Enough for both to get a clear view of each other, he supposed. It had struck him that the man's careful messages hadn't included any requests for photos – not that knowing someone's appearance had ever been a prerequisite for *him* to arrange an encounter. This greying man, slightly slouched, appeared not much more than a decade older than him. His cable knit sweater mostly hid his thickened frame, though his bald spot gleamed under the light when he turned to lay a knit blanket over the sofa. This was in his future, too; he had seen it in his family – this fading, this going to seed. The man motioned for him to sit, and he pitched himself onto the couch as his host glided wordlessly from the room.

He used the moment alone to strip to his white briefs, testing a few postures and stances that might best accentuate this muscle group or that. He tried dangling one arm off the couch, then a leg; he cast his head downward, chin nearly to his collarbone. He looked towards his obliques as though posing them a question; he fixed his eyes there as though they might answer. And he tried, as he often did, to leave his body entirely – to picture how he might look from this man's point of view. Although he hadn't been sketched before, this exercise in detachment was also one of familiarity: sitting inside a strange place, trying to embody someone else's fantasy.

The man returned clutching an unzipped pouch, an abundance of thick charcoal pencils sticking out, and a glass of water. He'd settled on a casual, almost haphazard, reclining position – his hands tucked behind his head to best display the deep well of his underarms. His pose projected the post-coital. It was his offering to this aging man, a subversion that might also be his triumph: the opportunity to capture the greatest intimacy without ever having engaged in the act that might precipitate it. He nestled into the cushions and relaxed his gaze into the middle distance as the man set to work.

'What's your name?'

The question shook him back into the room. If a man asked him anything about himself, it usually came at the beginning of an encounter. Now and again, he'd get the odd question after the act, but these were always the perfunctory, disinterested sort of inquiries – where his accent was from, what his plans were for the weekend – cast out solely to break the silence as he tied his shoelace or tucked in his shirt at the door. In either case, he always had a backstory prepared. It was, in some regard, the part he liked best – that he could be whoever he wanted to be, or, more precisely, whatever he imagined most closely hewed to the ideal of the man who had invited him.

But a question now? It unsettled him, like someone stopping unzipping his pants to ask the title of his grandmother's favourite song. He looked across at the man hunched over his sketchpad, starbursts of shading just visible along one edge of the page.

'Henry,' he said, trying not to let his speech affect his pose. 'My name is Henry.'

Henry had never uttered his real name before. Showing up at a relative stranger's house required a certain level of circumspection. But here he was, telling this man a most personal detail. And Henry found himself going on, too: about how moving to the city he thought he should had curdled into just surviving in it. About how a prestigious editing internship he'd been told he should fight for had morphed into the precarious gig work that wearied him.

'That's the laws of motion for you,' the man said. Henry couldn't see his face.

'What?'

'Newton. An object in motion tends to stay in motion.

Or the opposite,' the man continued. Henry suddenly felt a pervasive warmth, not so much an abrupt breeze as an accrued weight like he was in a sauna. He asked the man if it was all right if he took his underwear off, too. It was, he replied, if Henry returned to the same position.

As he stripped further, Henry stole a few glances. The man opened and closed his eyes as he shifted his hand about the page with sure strokes, seemingly moving his pencil without watching the paper. Henry liked the way the man squinted towards him, periodically holding two fingers near his right eye, as though viewing each part of him through a tiny monocle. It seemed likely some kind of exercise in scale, or perspective, but it made Henry feel like he was the sun: too hot or blinding to look at, let alone draw near.

The truth was that Henry did not quite know where to look from his vantage on the couch. He couldn't peer directly at the man for fear of breaking the reverie Henry tried to create for him. A full-length mirror hung on the far wall, but he didn't want to look there either. He'd once heard that a German word existed for something similar – something about being too worried about one's own appearance to entirely enjoy the pleasure of erotic connection. But he'd forgotten the phrase. Or maybe it had never existed. He tried to concentrate on the sound of the man's pencil on the paper; he tried to remember the art classes he'd peered in on as he walked past during the three terms before he'd dropped out. He'd always wondered about the models – where they came from, if they showed up every week. What it was like to be perceived, motionless, devoid of context, in such a cramped space.

Henry was especially determined not to look too directly at the cash sitting next to the sketchbook. Not that he hadn't spotted it. They had agreed on one hundred, even. Henry appreciated the man placing it in plain sight, but its prominence on the table also felt a touch vulgar, a touch explicit. Although, he'd also appreciated how candid the man had been about the money in his definitive little messages with his careful little punctuation. So many of his clients danced around that bit: that even if pleasure circumambulated their encounter, it was still, ultimately, a transaction. He felt himself growing hard.

One hundred was less than Henry would have liked. It was certainly less than he had been paid for an hour even just a couple years earlier. The opportunities had been greater then, there was no doubt. But that was before the message boards had been shut down; before the AI in the apps got good enough to kick him off for advertising 'services'. Sure, he'd briefly paid to post an ad on an escort page, but all the other men had been willing to do so much more than him. Plus, they'd all been younger. Or much fitter. Or, often, both much younger and much fitter. Suddenly he wasn't sure where to look – or, perhaps, to be seen. It wasn't so different from the editing gigs he scrounged together or his actor friends beginning to settle for bit parts in low-budget films, still part of the industry but not in the place they imagined they'd be.

His right thigh seized. Swinging his dangling leg up onto the couch for a measure of relief, he glimpsed in the mirror a puckering and creasing of his skin around his abdomen, like a snare hanging loose from a drum. He lowered his leg again even as his muscles constricted. He tried to distract himself watching the man dip his hand into the water and then drag it along the page, but he also tried to keep his eyes on the movement instead of the portrait itself. The work wasn't done; it didn't seem right to pass judgment on it yet.

'Do you want a drink?'

Before Henry could answer, the man leaned over and pulled two mini-bottles from a wall-mounted shelf. They were the same as the ones they served on airplanes, the ones he'd drunk on the flight in celebration of his move. He'd imagined champagne then but hadn't the money for it. Not that he did now either. He didn't think they even sold these things, but he reached for it anyway, grateful for the relief the movement provided. He massaged his tender thigh. He probably couldn't sit like this much longer, his legs flexed, his abs tensed.

'I can show it to you if you'd like?' the man asked as Henry screwed the cap off the bottle with his teeth. He remembered the man asking the question over text before he'd thrown on his coat and walked out into the rain.

'You're done already?' Henry didn't mean for his voice to modulate up as he answered a question by asking his own. The final word sounded like an accusation. Now that his leg was done cramping, part of him hoped the man needed longer to finish some of the finer details of the sketch. He could lay back down, and the man could get it all just right.

'You choose a point to put the pen down. Someone else declares its value then,' the man said, shrugging his shoulders and thrusting the sketchbook into Henry's free hand.

Henry opened the cover. The portrait was not at all what he had expected. His muscles seem slighter, less significant. His abdomen was neither loose nor taut – it was simply out of focus, as though submerged in a viscous pool. Only his head was defined. The striations in his forehead, their granularity upset him. Lines crumpled his face like etchings, and he saw a terrible brightness in his eyes. Henry thought he had been looking askance throughout the sitting, but the man seemed to have captured him mid-appraisal – assessing the proximity of some ambivalence, perhaps, but also of some kind of power. The sketch appeared as rough as it did bold.

The living room was quiet. Henry didn't mind the silence as he considered the work, just grateful the man didn't ask if he liked it. It was the one thing he couldn't stand a man asking after the fact. The question seemed like a trap. The truth was that sometimes he enjoyed himself and sometimes he didn't. Wasn't it this way for everyone? It was how he had ended up here – at this man's house, with his job, in his life. What else could he do now to shift it? He laid back down again on the couch, studying the dark shading along its margins, his cramp invisible on the page.

'The water technique is unusual,' the man said, pointing to his blurred thighs. 'Then again, maybe putting a pencil to a paper and trying to make it look like a fully realised human is unusual to begin with.' The man chuckled, a deep, assured vibration that soothed Henry.

'You know, you really are a natural at this,' the man said. He'd been told this before, but he'd always been suspicious, unsure whether this kind of work was really a skill at all. Maybe it was stupid. Or vapid. Or devoid in some measure. But part of him thought the ability to be projected upon was a virtue, an aspiration.

'You're very good, too,' Henry heard himself saying, and he meant it. He wasn't sure if he liked the portrait, but the skill in its creation was undeniable. 'How did you learn?' It was, he realised, the first question he'd asked the man.

'Not unlike you, I suspect. Just kept going until it felt

right,' he said. It was vague, but Henry was happy to hear it still, a dim acknowledgment of something shared between them. The man bundled up his pencils, clutched his glass, and left the room.

Henry sat alone, unsure what to do. He finally excused himself, apologizing to the empty room, and found his way through the dim corridor and into the bathroom. He swung the door only partially closed, revealing a spotless vanity. If the man walked past in the dark, Henry would grab him by the hand, he decided, and pull him up onto it. He'd pull him atop the bright enamel and press their bodies together in one swift motion.

Minutes passed in front of the mirror above the vanity before he noticed the glass of water. The man must have brought it into the bathroom when he finished the portrait. Henry rested his dick over the lip of the sink and poured the water over himself. It was still warm. He braced the mirror with one hand and washed with the other, his palm leaving a smudge of his own sweat on the glass. The man called to him, and Henry scuttled to the living room, ready to pull him down onto the couch, lead him into the bedroom, whatever he wanted.

'Do you want anything before you go?' the man asked, holding Henry's clothes.

The question shook him out of the room. He wanted to know what the man wanted. Maybe he could find out if he sat for another portrait. Perhaps the man would do another; perhaps he could stay here.

'Come again soon,' the man said, smiling as he ushered him back into the foyer. 'We can do another angle.' Henry tied his shoes wordlessly, and the man handed him the wad of bills along with his coat from the radiator.

The man tore a page from his notebook and thrust it toward him. 'You almost forgot my sketch. If you want it.'

Henry took it. He'd been sure the portrait was for the man, that he would keep it as a kind of relic, a prize. Henry had thought, not without a measure of pride, that the man would probably wank over it. Instead, he clutched it in his own hands, the paper thinner than he'd imagined.

Across the threshold, the man tried to hand Henry another twenty. He shook his head and gently pushed it back towards the man. He would be back, Henry assured him – assured both of them, he decided. Unsure of the exact way, he rifled in his pocket to fish out his phone as the man closed the door. The sketch flapped in the wind. Maybe he could fold it up and shove it into his wallet with the bills. Maybe it was like a currency only he could use. Henry looked at it once more, even surer now that it didn't really resemble him at all.

His phone buzzed. Another client, one who'd gone silent. He looked at his watch. Plenty of time to make it across the city. He'd already walked so far; what was a few more miles? Henry wondered what the next man might ask him as he peeled off his wet clothes in the entranceway.

Rounding onto a familiar street, the rain began again. He unzipped his coat just enough to tuck the sketch, uncreased, against his warm body.

Gaar Adams is a writer, educator and journalist whose reporting from the Middle East and South Asia has been featured in *The Atlantic, Rolling Stone,* and *Foreign Policy.* He is a former London Library Emerging Writer and his

debut – a narrative non-fiction book on queerness, migra-
tion, and belonging in the Middle East – will be published
by Harvill Secker in 2024. He holds a Doctorate of Fine
Arts from the University of Glasgow.

For Ezra – Libro Levi Bridgeman

I became a grandparent by accident
in the way that I wasn't prepared
but my son and his girlfriend might have been
I can't be sure

my grandson was born in November
a Sagittarius
he is chunky with rolly limbs like banh mi
and has brown watchful eyes
like he's been here before

my grandson is very content
he giggles like he took the best shot of vitamin D
and only cries
when he wants to eat or sleep or be changed

in the morning he makes coughing sounds
like a little newsreader
and he relishes cake tins and Henry the Hoover
and wheels and round things that turn

but I'm not sure how to tell him
that I, his grandparent, am non-binary so I'm
not really a grandfather or a grandmother but a
grand dandy

and sometimes I wear suits and vintage ties
and I have a short back 'n' sides
and I have had top surgery

I raised my son, my grandson's daddy, as my own
but my son didn't come out of me
so the whole bloodline thing doesn't work
only the nurture thing does
my son is like me, quite stubborn and artistic
and we both like stripey cats
and cartoons like Mr Ben

maybe my grandson will like these things too
and want to paint
or go on the stage
and eat a lot of potatoes and starchy things
and laugh at reality TV

one day, I might write a story just for my grandson
who comes from this rainbow family

or I could give him this poem
as way of explanation

Libro Levi Bridgeman Libro Levi has a Ph.D from UEA in Creative & Critical Writing where they were awarded the HSC Scholarship. BBC Radio 4 writing credits include: Caterpillars (2012), Dogfood Diary (2014) co-written with Charles Lambert). Theatre writing credits include: The Butch Monologues (2013–present day), short stories include: Letter To My Future Lover (F, M and Other, Knight Errant Press) XXX (*Queer Life, Queer Love*, Muswell Press). Libro Levi co-runs hotpencil press with Serge Nicholson publications include: Letter To My Little Queer Self (2021). Libro Levi is currently working on screen and TV plays. Their feature film Parker Parker (2022) is currently optioned by Creators Inc.

Epiphany – Sophia Blackwell

Christ the King and Lady Margaret's School present William Shakespeare's *Twelfth Night*: 15th December, 1998

Orsino, Duke of Illyria: Stephen Seward
Malvolio, Steward to Olivia: Craig Hewitt
Olivia, a Countess: Millie Thynne
Viola, sister to Sebastian: Nina Rushworth

I unbutton my suit for the last time, my fingers reluctant. It's the last day of term and possibly the last day of my relationship with Stephen Seward, the prettiest boy in the school across the street. I still need to tell him. It may ruin his Christmas, but I'm running out of time.

I miss my suit already. When she was pregnant, my mum was sure I was a boy. 'You were so big,' she said, 'and long! When they told me, I said, 'You're wrong, there must be some mistake. But there you were!' My mum might have been onto something, but anyway, here I am.

Wincing with a series of sharp pains, I tug my hair out of its lacquered bun. My mother's Greek, and you can see it in my hair, haloing out in an immovable mass that hair serums can only do so much for. I wipe off the rancid make-up that smells like someone's maiden aunt. ('The play was the usual Shakespeare guff they force us to endure on a regular basis, but Nina Rushworth is quite fit,' according to the first reviews from the boys' school.) I'd enjoyed being Viola, with Stephen waiting for me in the wings, my best friend Millie flirting with me as my Olivia, and Jasmine on my mind.

Jas Andrews. Jas, the golden girl with velvety skin while the rest of us stoically accepted our pallor and spots, super-cool Jas with her is-she-or-isn't-she haircut like Leonardo DiCaprio's curtains in Baz Luhrmann's *Romeo + Juliet*, our school's real Bible. Jas, two crucial years older, who left for Brighton last year and took a piece of me with her. Jas, who swore she'd see me on my last night, though I never saw her in the audience.

*

I'm no stranger to acting. First it was my accent, rubbing out glottal stops and learning to end half of my sentences with a question mark, like that Australian girl who fingered me in the toilets of the Glasshouse, the club that it's sometimes cool to go to and sometimes not, depending on which night it is. Then I had to learn not to look at girls, as though I was wearing blinkers in the changing rooms. I rechristened my on-and-off partners with male names – Johnny, Frank, Josh – but never Mike, the name of Millie's boyfriend. Mike, whose erect penis has been described to me in forensic detail. Scrotums aren't much to look at, apparently, but having a boyfriend is the most important thing. If you didn't have one, you might be – well, like *me*.

'Nina, I can see your nipples,' says Millie behind me as I swap my shirt for the black velvet Chipie dress that cost me a month's allowance.

'Yes, Millie, that would be because it's Baltic back here.' Backstage, the air is like breathing cold, wet towels. 'What is it with the boys' school and its complete lack of heating?'

'Sadism, probably. And you'd know all about that.' Millie is one of the seven people who knows I'm gay – or bi, or whatever, so she thinks I'm an expert on all things sexual. I worry about her telling the others, but somehow even when I told her it didn't feel like enough. Yes, I felt one of the lace-thin layers disappearing between me and the person I want to be some day, but I had hoped she'd suddenly understand all the parts of me I kept hidden, and that didn't happen.

It wasn't Millie's fault. She's just a sweet girl with parents who go to church twice a week. How could she know the important things? How I worry about dying alone, even though I'm only sixteen and still technically have a boyfriend? How my own body feels too unruly, too curvy, too short, and how I wish I could just unzip it and step out of it like an old school uniform?

At least it's Christmas. I can't wait to cry over made-for-TV movies and read Jasmine's precious letters from university with their little dancing stick-figures like Keith Haring drawings in the margins. I want to be silent, to expand again into my real, full self. I want to speak Greek with my grandmother and watch as she squints at the New Year cake, making sure I get the piece with the coin.

I hang my suit crookedly on the rack, seeing its long, streaky stitches and creases as the magic falls away from it, the pinholes and tucks where it was moulded to my body.

The first time Jas really saw me, I was wearing a suit for another play, some Ancient Greek thing where the jokes were supposed to be funnier than they were. She watched me adjusting my tie in the mirror as she came out of the toilet cubicle, and I felt warmth radiate through me – as powerful as panic, but much nicer. Unable to help it, we smiled at each other.

Then it was everything. It was mix-tapes and coffee from the twenty-four-hour cafe by the station, gritty and burned, offset with the chemical cream and powder of tiramisu. It was two-hour phone calls lying on the floor of my parents' study, meandering conversations that went nowhere and everywhere. It was grainy art-house cinema made by European people with mysterious depressions and it was poems we copied out for each other in handwriting that wasn't quite our own, each one a masterclass in avoiding the three words we couldn't say, each one a wreath laid around an absence.

'Come on,' says Millie. 'I think I can smell mulled wine. And now the show's over, you can dump Stephen without cocking it all up.'

*

'Nina!' Stephen comes up to me in the boys' school hall, which smells particularly ripe this evening, the sweaty, cub-like smell of the boys mingling with our parents' perfumes and aftershave, the odd hint of cold air. 'My Viola.'

He's hamming it up for the boys, who are snickering around him. 'Go on, Steve-o!' one of them shouts. One or two of the boys, the play's lesser lords, hyped up on their performances, sing a chant I've heard around the playing fields, 'Steve-o, put on a lap-dance show! Wiggle wiggle! Jingle jingle! Steve-o!'

He looks at me as if to say, 'You see what I have to put up with.' It's a shame to dump someone who looks so good in a suit. The other boys always look as though they're about to take their Confirmation, or that they're on remand from the nearest prison. Stephen, on the other hand, always looks sharp, his dark hair styled in an almost-quiff, his canines slightly pointed. I always liked that about him. He's hungry for something, but I don't think it's me.

'You were great,' I say, as he shoos his friends away from us. 'Getting ready for the Footlights?'

'Oh, God!' The campness comes back into his voice. 'I should be so lucky! You know I made a hash of my GCSEs last year. Not what you need, when you want to be a doctor.'

'I thought you wanted to be an actor.'

He shrugs. 'Bit of both, maybe. I might go to medical school and do plays on the side. In fact, I just got asked to be in the New Year show at the church hall. I don't suppose you fancy coming. I'll be wearing a dress for most of it.'

'Sounds perfect,' I say, and he cracks a reluctant smile. 'What does your mother think about it?' Stephen's mother is a pillar of the community, who hasn't really got the memo about her son. His eyes slide towards her, small and sober in her square-shouldered grey jacket.

'Oh, she loves it,' he says quietly. 'So long as I don't bring the dress home.'

'Stephen, I wanted to . . .'

'Hold that thought.' He's already gone, grabbing one of the other actors' arms, like a proper celebrity. It used to drive me mad when I still thought I fancied him. He does rush everywhere, and I don't think he means anything malicious by it. I used to like watching him in motion. When we got together, we were standing on opposite train platforms after a rehearsal, and he signalled to me – *wait*. I remember smiling as he ran up the stairs, knowing what he was going to say, knowing that I'd been chosen.

I get a white foam cup of lukewarm mulled wine and sit down next to Millie, who's looking beautifully pre-Raphaelite in her own black dress. 'She'll come,' she says, reading my mind. 'Have you told him yet?'

'No, he buggered off to talk to someone more important as usual.'

'Nina.' She taps her foam cup against mine. 'No one is more important than you. Apart from me, I've got a hipflask.'

*

The party's winding down and the school corridors are getting that slightly haunted, hollow look in the winter dark. I convince Millie to wait for me in the pub and make a call in the phone box by the station. I know Jas's number by heart, and I know she should be home from college now. When I've thought about her in the past week, I've thought of all those people in Christmas songs, travelling home, everyone going where they need to be.

Her voice sounds flat and clogged. 'Nina. I was going to come, but I had a fight with my dad. You know what he's like. I ended up going on a bender with Aoife last night . . .'

'What, the one you used to . . .'

'Oh God, Nina, nothing happened! Why do you always think that? We're just mates, that's all. Went down the Blue Bar, did some shots, got paralytic . . .'

'You could have asked me.'

'I know. I should have. But I'm not sure I can see you this time round.'

'What, you could go to Blue Bar, but you can't see me?'

'I'm skint. Besides, this thing with my dad ... I'm just lying low, going as soon as Christmas is over.'

'I'll pay for you.' I swallow hard. 'I've got money.'

'I can't let you do that. You're younger than me. It feels wrong.'

'I didn't make you spend that money on shots!'

Jas is silent for a while. I can hear her breathing. 'Maybe just not this time, OK? Look, you know how much I care about you. I'm just in a weird place now and I don't really want you to see me like this.' She laughs, but it sounds hollow. 'I know you look up to me, sort of, or at any rate you did. I don't know why. You're so special, Nina. When are you going to see I'm just a mess?'

'I don't care what you are,' I say. 'I want to see you.'

When did this stop being fun? When did I stop being able to say no to her? I keep thinking about when that moment might have been. I don't know when she stopped seeing me as someone she might want and started seeing me as an annoying kid who no longer has a place in her life.

'Look,' she says after a while.

And then she tells me about her new girlfriend, Stephanie, who's reading PPE. I'm not sure what that is but I don't feel like this is the right time to ask.

I don't know how the rest of the conversation goes, but I find myself standing at the station like someone in one of our indie anthems, wishing I smoked. I remember Stephen, running up the platform towards me. Sod it, maybe I'll give him another go. It is Christmas.

As I walk past the church on the corner and up towards the pub, I see two figures leaning against the church wall. Two boys, one in a thick black jacket, collar pulled high and a beanie hat as though his main goal tonight was anonymity, and one without a coat, still in the light summer jacket he always wears to run from place to place. My boyfriend, Stephen Seward, is getting off with Malvolio.

He sees me before I can do anything. 'Sorry,' I say, pointlessly.

'Oh God. Nina. Wait!' he splutters, though I'm not moving. Craig, Malvolio, wipes his mouth and stands next to Stephen, his eyes still rimmed with black mascara from the show.

Seeing him like this is strangely painful, though I know my affections have also been elsewhere. 'It's OK,' I say. 'It's all right.'

'Could you not . . .' he swallows. 'I know this is a lot to ask but could you please not tell anyone? You can hate me if you like – I haven't always been good to you, it doesn't . . . weirdly, it doesn't mean I don't love you, just not . . .'

'Stephen,' I say. 'I'm like you.'

'Well, yes, that's why we . . .'

'No, you're not listening.' I think of Jas, my hands on the silk tie as I turned around to look at her. There may well be others who will look at me that way. I just need to find them, and to do that I have to be the person I think I am, under all this hair and cheap velvet. 'I am just like you, Stephen,' I say slowly. 'Are you getting it now?'

'I told you she didn't fancy you,' says Craig. Stephen and I look into each other's eyes, knowing it doesn't matter now whether I do or not. 'Come on. Let's go to the pub.'

*

On New Year's Eve, my dad gives me a lift to Stephen's show, and I watch him sparkle on stage in a big yellow frock, stopping the show. Even when he sees me in the crowd, his face doesn't waver. A few days later, he calls me and tells me he's got just the part for me in a new show he's directing. 'And no showmance this time,' he tells me. His show's set in the 1920s. It gives me the excuse I need, whether it happens in the end or not.

Before I go back to school, we go to my grandmother's house for lunch, and I get the piece of cake with the coin inside and act surprised. In the evening, I find myself in a hair salon in town. The young woman behind me in the mirror is just my type, with cayenne-coloured hair and an undercut, a lizard tattoo peeking up at me from the waist-band of her jeans.

She holds my hair, the two dark curtains I once hid behind, doubtfully in her hands. 'All of it?'

'Yes,' I say, and then, 'Please.'

I sit back in the busy, steamy salon on the unremarkable fifth day of January, and watch as the damp black weight falls away, each snip bringing me closer to the person I suspected I might be. For the last few minutes, I don't look – I close my eyes, and she asks me if I'm all right. *Yes,* I say inside myself. *Yes.*

'Nothing's forever,' she says quickly, clearly thinking I'm freaking out about my hair.

'I know,' I say, and open my eyes. I see a boy, a girl, a man, a woman; all of it in one sleek-haired, open-eyed body walking into the streets of a new world.

The face in the mirror smiles, and something inside me smiles back.

Sophia Blackwell has published three poetry collections and a novel. Her work has been anthologised by Bloodaxe, Nine Arches and The Emma Press. She hosts LGBT+ arts programmes on Resonance FM, and she was co-host and producer of the Polari Podcast. Her first non-fiction book, *The Poetry Writers' Handbook*, was published by Bloomsbury in Autumn 2022.

Doing Admin in Gaza –
Sharon Shaw

'Passing is the means through which the violence of assimilation takes place.' I thought about this aphorism coined by M.B. Sycamore as I found myself, with my complicated ethnicity, skin fade and tattooed forearms standing in front of a group of heavily armed Israeli teenagers at the Erez Crossing, the only foot crossing into Gaza from Israel.

I was travelling with a young English colleague fresh to the industry, leading him through a baptism of sorts into the kind of work he'd unwittingly signed up for. The Erez Crossing looks on the Israeli side like a regular international terminal, clearly capable of ferrying tens of thousands of people from one side to another, but with no more than four people there including myself it felt uncanny. I was ushered into a pen and met by a young officer in a towering cubicle.

'What's your father's first name?'

'Richard.'

'and his father?'

'Jack.'

Her mobile buzzed and illuminated the screensaver, a

painfully staged selfie of her hugging what I assumed was her boyfriend.

'What about his father?' she kept on, her nails clacking against the phone as she typed out a swift response to a text.

'Honestly, I have no idea.'

I was unsure if she'd been expecting a Mohammed or a Moshe but there wasn't one to give so she eventually waved me through.

My colleague was waiting for me, he passed security more easily. He looked like the 'before' version of the other two men waiting to get through the border. They were biding their time outside the terminal, both weather-beaten with sun-bleached roguish hair tucked behind their ears, same black wraparound glasses on their heads, same cigarette burning down between their fingers on the same tanned arm.

The strict security and customs interventions included a gauntlet of tight, full-body turnstiles. My heavy backpack was cutting into my shoulders, and I was grateful to find a Palestinian man at what seemed like a bustling rest stop in the middle of nowhere, populated with men clearly used to waiting. They sat chain smoking, sipping Pepsi and cooling off under a tarp. He would minibus us to the final checkpoint on the other side for a mere five shekels and I could avoid the fifteen-minute walk in the heat through an endless narrow caged walkway that wove its way through a no man's land of sand and rubble.

There isn't a list or website you can refer to regarding what is or isn't permitted into Gaza, so packing a bag had not been simple. There is partial list on the internet alleg-edly cobbled together by NGOs. I had with me the clothes on my back and a bag containing:

x2 socks
x1 Passport
x1 press card
x1 flak jacket
x1 headscarf
x1 credit card
x2 ear defenders
x1 ballistic helmet
x1 groin protector
x1200 Israeli Shekels
x1 tube of Jelly Bellys
x1 regular sunglasses
x1 phone and charger
x1 ballistic sunglasses
x2 pairs of underwear
x1 anti-aging night cream
x1 Government Press card
x1 Ventolin asthma inhaler
x2 giant packets of chocolate
x1 toothbrush and toothpaste
x1 battery pack charged with 24 re-charges
x1 water bottle with military issue water filter

The final checkpoint was a series of makeshift 'offices', with shipping crates dotted haphazardly around a sandy clearing. I was grateful to find my Gazan colleague waiting to guide us from cabin to cabin, each one containing serious men, with serious beards. Unsmiling at first, they would ask a series of questions, rustle paperwork but when moved to, gesture and laugh. I was relieved I was not more heavily scrutinised. My background is complicated to say the least, having immediate family that are Catholic, Muslim and

Jewish. I watched my colleague try to persuade these serious men that he'd never been in the military.

I was extremely conscious I was sitting in a shoebox with agents of what many consider to be a terrorist organisation, in a place where homosexuality is illegal. Tattoos and short hair on women are not exactly a definitive mark of the queer, but neither are they a conversation starter with the deeply religious. Being a lesbian is not a 'real' thing in the Strip, but it is not protected either.

I only saw one other woman, well-dressed and incredibly composed. She entered the cabin, sat down and knowing the drill she made herself comfortable. She smiled at me with that look of solidarity reserved for other women in rooms such as these and then looked away, busying herself with something or other in the room she pretended to find fascinating.

Entry approved, I clambered into an armoured vehicle where my colleague told me that they didn't ask me a lot of questions because my first application for entry had been denied and had to be resubmitted with a lot more detail. When I asked why, he turned and looked at me closely, to make sure I wouldn't be offended.

'They thought you looked like a man: your hair is so short, and it doesn't help that your name here is an insult,' he said smiling.

We were all silent before falling about in fits of laughter.

The car was heavily re-enforced, I felt trapped behind the bullet-proof glass. I could see out, but people couldn't see in, almost like I was on some kind of safari but completely unsure of what exactly I was being protected from. We looked for somewhere to stop: the guys wanted to buy cigarettes, so we pulled in behind a donkey and cart laden with oranges next to a sneaker shop selling FILAs and Nikes sitting in sun-faded rows. It was run by boys with great haircuts whose store and occupants would have looked completely at home in Hackney.

We smoked and chatted as I looked in at the bookshop next door selling colourful paperbacks, laid out in the window mosaic-style, with a copy of Orwell's *1984* front and centre.

My job is to manage international locations for an international broadcaster. I help to make sure that the Palestinian men that operate this outpost have what they need to do the jobs they do. That is, to share their own stories and those of the over two million other Gazans living within 141 square miles of the most mind-boggling situation humanity could ever have negotiated itself into. They work from their discrete location, telling their side of the story, whilst my other friends and colleagues on the other side of the border, the barrier, the wall, whatever term your politics or your heritage allow you to call it, tell theirs.

My colleagues told me when I arrived that I didn't need to wear a headscarf, but I was conscious of standing out. The rationale was to not cause any confusion. When I wear a headscarf, I look like I was born for it, but the rest of me does not; the incongruity could cause problems best avoided if my appearance and my behaviour didn't match expectation.

'It is best they see you as a westerner.'

'This is not Ramallah, I guess.'

'No, it is not.'

I headed off to a meeting with a local broadcaster and was entertained warmly from the moment I arrived. The editor was a lovely man in his fifties, he poured us little cups of thick syrupy coffee and told me a magically off-colour joke about the Pope and Bill Clinton whilst his colleague took himself off to pray. I told him about the reaction my name 'Sharon' had been getting due to the association with the 11th Prime Minister of Israel. He laughed.

'Let me tell you a story. Have you ever heard the joke about the family known as the Sharameet?'

'I am unfamiliar with that one,' I blushed, 'but I think that it's the plural for . . .' I hesitated; '. . . er, a lady of the night?'

I wondered if any of this exchange would have happened if I'd been sitting opposite him in a dress.

'Precisely, you are correct.'

'I love a joke, tell me.'

So, this family, The Sharameets, this was their name. There was Mr Sharameet, Mrs Sharameet, all their Sharameet children and Sharameet aunts and uncles. This was of course a heavy name to carry, and the children suffered in school, people would laugh and point when they passed. Thankfully their business didn't suffer too much: the name was something of a draw, but money isn't everything, and it made them feel shame. One day Mr Sharameet, fed up of this constant battle for his dignity, decided he would change his name to improve his family's standing. He didn't have to think hard about what he would choose. He went for 'al Sheikh', a name fit for a king. He planned a large party, sent out announcements, they even sacrificed an animal. Everyone came, and they danced, they ate, and everyone congratulated the family on the festivities. The local baker, a friend of the family was also there, he had a wonderful time. Full of tea and rich meat, he finally left for home but on his way, he bumped into a customer.

'Where have you been this evening my friend?'

'Why, I've been at a lovely party at the house of the Sharameets,' the baker said.

'They tried to be something they weren't, bless them,' I said.

The editor laughed right at me.

'Save your pity for the real "Al Sheikh" family! Now everywhere they go, everyone thinks they are actually the Sharameets!'

We wandered out to the roof for a cigarette; there was a lot of coffee and a lot of cigarettes in this place. It was a clear day, I could see most of the city, a sprawl of densely packed grey pock-marked buildings, most no more than half a dozen stories high. Vacant lots, between rows of buildings, sat empty not by design but by destruction. The psycho-geography of this place seemed completely unknowable to outsiders. The sandy gaps, perhaps once places of strategic importance which exist now only in memory.

When I got back to the hotel it was dark. A wedding had taken over the hotel and filled it with beautifully dressed people and sparkling decorations. A lot of things in this city don't work, lie broken, half-mended, waiting until supplies can be found. But in this hotel, they were keeping up the illusion.

The back of the bedrooms opened out onto a covered terrace; my English colleague and I met for dinner, eager to talk about our day. The wedding party were congregated in the huge hall below us. We collapsed into a huge, cushioned wicker sofa and ate modestly, scoffing *Kibbeh*: bulgur wheat fried into spindle shapes filled with meat and spices, which we dipped into a bowl of hummus whilst we watched the festivities.

I left the next day. Back in Israel, my luggage arrived, spat out of a conveyor emerging from an enormous windowless block. Every single item was out of place, including my underwear, which arrived gussets turned out. I made a mental note to remember what a good hiding place a gusset was. I felt like a fraud dragging my flak jacket around emblazoned with its Velcro PRESS patch. I was relieved when I managed to quickly work it back into my bag as I watched a young Palestinian boy next to me, gaunt and bald, waiting for his own bag. It wasn't a huge leap to understand his family had managed to get him and his father a permit to leave for cancer treatment. His father hovering near him was wordlessly urging him to sit down. I thought about the list of prohibited items not permitted to be taken over the foot crossing, and then understood that nuclear scanning equipment or even radiotherapy may not have been available in Gaza. A card, a single plastic press pass about 2" by 3", and a British passport allowed me to pass back and forth across this border and I knew they had no such luxury.

Whilst waiting for my colleague I noticed a piece of something shiny poking out from the sole of my shoe: a tenacious sliver of wedding decoration had worked its way into a groove and made it over the border. I thought about the history of this place. You can feel it all around you, like an interminable loop playing over the present. I thought about the night before, all bright twirling skirts and sequined glare. I'd eaten and I'd watched. I'd watched the wedding party eat. I'd watched them dance. I'd watched as the power went out and the glass windows of the grand building shook violently, from a rocket attack a few miles away. I watched as the people kept dancing.

Sharon Shaw, born in London, is of Persian/Angolan/Portuguese extraction. She's worked in film and reality TV in LA and London and currently works across the Middle East, Central Asia and the Caucasus for a major broadcaster. She holds a Master's in Creative Writing from Birkbeck and is working on her first novel.

Deep Black Ice — Peter Mitchell

In memory of my partner,
Don Campbell

1.
The wind scatters the seeds
of the silent
       into the nameless. Now,
  as always, there is much
          that is never understood.

2.
The hands of the clock are stuck.
  The certainties
       of time are a forfeit
   as days become
         vanishing points.

3.
Anger thunders from a diseased husk.
I want curious tongues cut out,
mouths glued shut.
    No lips, no names.

4.

Grief is a plump fruit.
My body is a pear as it shrivels to a core.

5.
Days are counted as fingers
enclose the sweet tingle
of bourbon
& coke & ice.
Memories blur to word-smears.

6.
I am buried
In deep   black   ice,
a vapour of cold
rising

like a gift.

7.
The line of vision
goes towards

the book of tomorrow.
Flyspecks dot
these pages.

8.
Dim holograms, winters
of rust. The flickering
                dark
                            scattergrams
pinheads
        of   conviction.

9.
For now,
I bake our favourite date scones,
      your mother's recipe in front of me.
            Your remembered smiles
appreciate
                  this cemetery air.

———————————————

Peter Mitchell (he/him/his) lives in Lismore on Widjabul/
Wia-bul Country, Bundjalung Nation, and writes across all
narrative forms. His writing has appeared or is forthcom-
ing in international and national journals and anthologies.
He has authored two poetry chapbooks, *Conspiracy of Skin*
(Ginninderra Press, 2018) and *The Scarlet Moment* (Picaro
Press, 2009). *Conspiracy of Skin* was Highly Commended in
the 2019 Wesley Michel Wright Prize for Poetry.In 2022,
he was Longlisted for the Flying Islands Poetry Prize.
www.peter-mitchell.com.au , Insta: @petermitchell546
FB: @Peter Mitchell Wordsmith

Hotel Outcall – Rab Green

London 2017

On the 10th floor of the St Giles Hotel, the lift takes ages to come. When it finally does, there's a young fidgety lad inside.

The big button for LOBBY is already pressed. He asks,
Is that for the ground floor?
Yeah, are you looking to go out?
Yeah.
Yeah, that's the one.
OK, I wasn't sure.
The softness and worry in his voice, the age of him, maybe twenty years younger than me.

And as the lift starts to move, I take in: the strong smell of his cologne, his skinny stone-washed jeans, the stubble on his jaw and cheeks, his shaved upper lip. I wonder if he was in the hotel for the same reason I was.

But I feel unfriendly and spent, unwilling and a little too guarded to properly engage. Not quite confident enough, not quite sure who I'd be, to turn and ask him how his evening is going.

When the lift doors open at the lobby, he steps out first, but stops, falters. I step out of the lift behind him, almost put my arm around him, almost put my hand on the small of his back,

It's this way.

OK.

You're wanting to get to the street?

Yeah. I thought I'd never get out of this hotel.

I smile and think: we'll talk more when we get down the steps or out the glass doors or onto the street. But he's keeping ahead of me, speeding up and I'm maybe only ten seconds behind him when he turns the corner onto Tottenham Court Road, and it's enough to lose sight of him, by the time I've followed him round the corner, in amongst the people milling around the tube station entrance and the crowd from a theatre show, heading home.

Rab Green is a Scottish writer and artist living in London. He has work published in print by Sidekick Books and Acid Bath Publishing, and online by Factory Theatre Workshop, t'Art and Chewboy Productions. He has also had work included in *Truth and Lies: An Anthology of Writing and Art by Sex Workers*, published by Arika. He can be found at: rabgreen.co.uk.

I Fell in Love with a Boy Who Then Blocked Me on Grindr –
Stanley Iyanu

Last night, you sent shockwaves through me
and I felt the tremors of three heartbeats that
soared through the silence – it cocooned me,
where you started and I began, like a constant
interwoven thread, upended but still complete.

Tomorrow, I'll marry that boy,
delete those apps and move to Clapham.
I'll dye my hair, get a French bulldog,
a personal trainer. Tomorrow, he'll block
me and I'll be back on those apps, *again*.

Tomorrow, I'll marry that boy,
delete those apps and move to Shoreditch.
Paint myself in tattoos, join a ska band,
get a Doberman. Tomorrow, he'll block
me and I'll be back on those apps again.

Tomorrow, I'll marry that boy,
delete those apps and move to Notting Hill.
Take up Pilates, fill my days with flower-arranging,
    and
Brutalist architecture. Tomorrow, he'll block
me and I'll be back on those apps again.

In a year's time, I wonder if I'll *still* be heartbroken,
wonder if his absence will *still* feel like a drought –
if the aching will *finally* cease, if the cavity will close by
    itself.
Wonder if I'll find answers to questions or if I will
stop searching for them, cradle the hurt, let things be.

The day tastes like umami,
smells like roasted black coffee or cold halloumi,
No! it tastes like stilted goodbyes and quiet yearning,
an unresolved ending for things left unsaid   like the
conversation behind uneasy stares, unuttered words.

Today, I won't deny my love for you –
how your loss felt like rejection,
how your eyes bore holes into me,
how I *still* want you with your all conflicts and
    complications –
well, parts of me do … might always do.

One day, we'll find love again – I have this warped
    daydream:
I'd be your safe space and you'd be my refuge.
We'd make a home out of broken hearts and hard lessons;

paste over our trauma and heal our old wounds. We'd
   argue,
fuck to our hearts content but be madly, deeply in this.
   This I promise you

Stanley Iyanu is a performance poet and writer from
London. He has performed across the UK, most notably
for Apples & Snakes, BBC Radio London and for the
Cheltenham Literature Festival. His debut poetry pamphlet
is called *My Achilles*, published by Burning Eye Press in
Autumn 2023.

Nobody's Sons – Jonathan Pizarro

Abdel said to wait for him by the *frontera* where the cars queue to cross into Spain. Marco walks down the lanes and hills of Upper Town. Down to where the land gets flat. Across to the place agreed. A patch of grass next to the barbed wire fence. Empty cigarette cartons at his feet. Ripped up and discarded by those who cross from Gibraltar back into Spain. Loose packets of tobacco padded under their clothes. Brilliant blue sky against the towering *palmeras* on the other side.

Marco spots Abdel on his red moto weaving through the traffic. Buzzing like a wasp. Getting closer. Abdel beeps, stops and throws Marco a helmet, tells him to get on. Hands placed at Abdel's hips. Fingers against the hardness of bones through shorts. He wants to slide his hands further down and feel the warmth between Abdel's legs. And the curve of his neck under the half-helmet so close to Marco's lips as they make it to the passport control.

The Spanish guard waves his hand. A signal for the vehicle to stop. *Los cascos*, he says. Monotone. He doesn't look at them directly. They pull off their helmets. *El motor*, he orders. Abdel turns the key to switch off the engine. Marco looks at the man dressed in green military uniform. The aviators keeping out all the light. The baton against his muscular thigh. A holstered gun protrudes on the opposite side. Trousers tight. Black boots laced up to the ankle. Chest bursting out of a shirt unbuttoned down to a thin golden crucifix.

The guard asks for their ID cards. He holds them up and checks the photographs against Marco and Abdel's faces. Marco notices the faint patch of sweat under the guard's arms. He must smell of tobacco and whisky. Of one of those sports deodorants for men with the tribal design.

Marco looks away. The impression of nonchalance. Like this was something that happened all the time. It's what Abdel told him to do if they got stopped. If you looked unemotional, slightly bored, you'd be fine. He focuses on the border fence. The rows of cars waiting inspection go forward at the pace of a snail. Motos and bicycles in their own separate pile. Pedestrians on the pavement show their documentation to a bored-looking guard in a kiosk who barely looks up from his newspaper. Another guard rifles through shopping bags and purses. Some people are marched into a building for more intimate searches. Drivers pull up boot doors. Batons are pointed at sections. An unspoken instruction to open. All the places possible to hide contraband are uncovered.

The guard tells them to get off the moto. He gestures for them to lift the compartment under the seat. One hand on his hip like he couldn't care less even though he's asked for this. He pushes the towels to one side. Open this bag, he barks. He sees the cans of beer and checks the ID cards again. He flips the cards over. Like they're the first ones he's ever seen. A relic of a foreign country.

Marco wonders where Gibraltar ends, where Spain begins. Is it Spain when they're let go, drive up the road past the checkpoint and join the main road up the coastline? Or is it now? This feels more like an in-between place. Their continuing journey dependent on the whims of this man. On how gracious he may be feeling towards the population on the other side of the line, whom he probably thinks took land three hundred years ago that belongs to his nation. Or he's just a man with bills to pay and children to feed and a wife to support. A man who wants to go for lunch. For a smoke. To finish his shift before the day gets hotter.

He lets them go with another wave. They climb back on. Abdel brings the moto to life. Hands onto hips. Legs spread, fitting into each other. When they pass the control area completely, Marco slips both hands around Abdel's waist and pulls himself closer.

Abdel turns left and out past the small stretch by the coach park and the Radio Taxi rank. He accelerates onto the main road and joins the traffic. Towards the sea. The Rock on their right at a distance behind the border fence that goes on and on until it ends Eastern Beach on the Gibraltar side and transforms into Playa de La Atunara on the Spanish side. The same water, the same land, but that line between them with the posts and the wire and the security cameras changes everything.

They turn again. Leaning into the road. Marco holds on tighter. He feels Abdel's stomach muscles contract and relax through the T-shirt. Along the *playa* with the wooden fishing boats in the sand. The *chiringuitos* and restaurants closed until noon. The *playa* deserted for now, apart from a group of men pushing a boat down to the waves. Another group spreading out their nets wide across the ground to let them dry after a night of them in the open sea.

They pass people walking up and down the Paseo Maritimo. Old couples hunched over, arm in arm. A man with a dog. A woman pulling her *carro* behind her on the way to the Wednesday *mercadillo*. Another man sits on a bench, smoking a pipe. The sun fully out of the water. The heat dry and tangible already on this August morning. And these people like reels of film they'll never see again. Snapshots of strangers. Who don't look up at two boys on a moto speeding along the street, one of them clutched tight to the other from behind. Here they are. Nobody's sons.

They reach the small church at the end of the *playa*. Its whitewashed walls shimmering. Doors thrown open. A statue of the Virgin in an alcove by the road. A burst of flowers red, white, and yellow at her feet. Marco puts his chin against Abdel's back. He feels it tense with the brakes and turns and acceleration. The fresh scent of Abdel's perfume. The rise and fall of his breathing. He kisses him between the shoulder blades.

At some point, they are far enough up the coast that they turn a curve and Gibraltar disappears behind them completely.

They sit on a spread-out blanket by the shore. The sun is high now and shimmers across the water. The Mediterranean flat as a plate. No land on the horizon. Abdel tells Marco it would be Algeria. Marco doesn't know anything about Algeria. An invisible country to their eyes.

The tide is lazy. Exhausted at the perpetual action of millennia. The traffic buzzes from the road above them.

Hidden by a tangle of trees and bushes that make this *cala* private. They're alone. Their hands meet. The thrill of leaving them where they are. Together. Not pulling away. Abdel squeezes. Marco squeezes tighter in return. They look at each other and smile. They kiss. They linger.

Noon. Abdel puts down his beer and pulls off his T-shirt. Unbuckles his shorts. Pulls them down in a swooping motion. He runs across the burning sand and jumps in. The elegant arch of his tanned body against the blue disappears into the water. When he comes up for air, he holds an arm out to Marco and says, *niño*, if you don't come in, I'll go there and bring you in with all your clothes, eh. Marco strips down to his underwear too and follows. Under the water. He slips between Abdel's legs. He comes up on the other side and is greeted with a kiss. Arms around his neck and down his back. His in symmetry.

Abdel's arm around his slick, wet waist. He holds Marco against his body as they stand in the shallows. He bites softly on Marco's lower lip. One hand slips further down the curve of his back and through the waistband of Marco's underwear. Marco opens his eyes and pulls away. He turns and looks at the path they came down to the *cala* from. Then towards the horizon. Like the boats would be out on patrol. Abdel's hand on his jaw. He turns Marco's head towards him. Abdel's deep green olive eyes. It's OK here, he says. *No pasa nada.* It's OK. Marco submits.

Hands inside. Between wet cotton and skin. The increasing speed of their motion creates small ripples on the surface. They give in. They push into themselves. Harder. Chest to chest. The tightness of an orgasm. They moan into the echo of each other's mouths.

Out here in the open under the sky with the light of the sun on them. No shadows. The entire sea for them alone.

Marco weightless. Face down. The sound of his arms cutting through the water muffled in his ears. His blurred vision. The sand on the seabed moving side to side. Shells and algae dragged along with it. A small group of fish fight against what to them is a ferocious tide.

He turns on his back. His head and shoulders and feet bobbing. The sudden harsh light in his eyes mixed with the sting of saltwater. His lungs ache from holding his breath. He gasps.

He rubs his face and pushes his hair back. He looks around at the horizon. A couple of small boats pass. A flock of seagulls so far away they look like a child's drawing of birds in the shape of a V.

Abdel basks. Spread out on a large rock. His head tilted up to the heat of the sun. Eyes closed. His back arched. Legs flat against the limestone. Abdel in the sunlight. Illuminated. The angle of his jaw. His collarbone. The roundness of his shoulders. A gold chain glints against his chest. The small fuzz of hair down to his navel. The perfect roundness of his small dark nipples. The tight muscles of his thighs. The careless gesture of his feet set apart. The promising roundness of his bulge in the black briefs.

Abdel opens his eyes and looks out at the water. He lifts a hand. Marco swims towards him.

Afternoon. Side by side. Underwear pushed down enough that their bare skin touches. Still clammy and cool from their swim. Heads resting on their palms. They look up at the sky. Soft white clouds roll in. It makes the breeze feel colder. Abdel props himself up on an elbow and trails fingers down Marco's side. Marco shivers. Abdel grins. Small patches of salt dry on his skin making patterns like maps of ancient worlds.

We could live here, Marco says. We could stay.

The portable radio sounds fuzzy. The song cuts out. A woman with a deep voice. Something about breathing. Abdel raises an arm. Marco moves into the concave of Abdel's armpit. A rose tattoo on his side. It blooms between his ribs. Marco kisses it. Sharp rasp of seawater and the memory of CK One and the cotton freshness promise of deodorant. And somewhere in there, Abdel's own scent. That pure, natural private smell that Marco breathes in because it's all for him. Between Abdel's legs when they fuck. Or in the middle of the night when he reaches out to hold him tighter and he puts his face close and just breathes in.

A ver, where would we live? Abdel asks. Marco feels the bass of his voice travelling through his bones. Under that rock? In the sea?

Marco closes his eyes. In a house, he replies. Just a small one. Close to here. *Ahí arriba,* up on the hills. We could spend every summer here in our secret *playa.*

On the drive up, Marco spotted the houses that were on the other side of the road. Little white or salmon squares with terracotta roofs were dotted around and overlooking the sea. With olive trees. Bursts of bougainvillea. The closest neighbour a ten-minute walk away. Nobody stacked on top of each other peering over the wall asking questions and making judgements. Every evening they could watch the sun dip into the water. No other city or mass of land.

Just the regular and dependable rhythm of the days and the nights and the tides.

They wake up from sleep. Their skin like clay in an oven. Marco kisses Abdel on the chest. He feels Abdel's lips on the crown of his head. Abdel's hand reaches into his hair. He tangles it between his fingers and pulls. A murmur. Marco's hand up the softness of Abdel's inner thigh. He feels Abdel harden. He rubs against the cotton. Teasing. The strain as pleasurable as the release. Abdel puts a hand on Marco's chin to tilt his head upward. He studies it, surprised.

Marco, *niño*, when did you get that scar? he asks. A raised thread on the jawline. Slightly paler. I think it was in the bath, Marco replies. When I was very *chico*. I fell. *No se*. I don't remember. I forgot I had it.

How can you forget you have a scar?

Marco shrugs. Annoyed at the interruption. They kiss. Open mouthed. Parting wider. Like there was a fear that either one of them could disappear at any moment and the other would starve for the rest of their life.

Evening. A woman walks down the path. Determined. All the way to the shore. They put their underwear on in a hurry. She doesn't look. But they look at her. The sky in the beginnings of a smouldering orange. She pulls at her ponytail. Grey hair releases as she waves it around. It settles. Limp. All the way down to the small of her back. She pulls at one side of her loose summer dress, and it slips down to her ankles. She stands there naked and walks into the water until she is fully immersed.

They pack away their things. The woman swims across the length of the *cala*. A disciplined breaststroke. When she gets to where it's shallow enough, she stands. Half her naked body out of the water. She looks at them. Before they turn to leave, they watch the sun set behind her. She waves at them. She smiles.

They wave back.

Jonathan Pizarro is a Queer Gibraltarian writer. His short fiction has been featured in *Popshot*, *Litro* and *Queerlings* amongst others, and has been shortlisted for both the 2021 Aurora Prize and the 2022 Commonwealth Prize. His stories deal with Queer desire, the Mediterranean, language, borders, and the aftermath of Empire. He is currently working on his forthcoming debut novel.

The Aftermath – Reanna Valentine

Last night, I drained quick   like a shallow bath
This morning, I've been filled   in most of the possible
    ways   or will be
Rubbing love onto the covers of other people's
    books   damp bedsheets
I am a used, spoiled, plump little cloud   curled happy
I don't even smell like me   intoxicating   oh, the
    combinations
The dirt under my fingernails   the parts of him on me

Gone all vapour floppy   I smile to myself mildly
His cum invisibly   soaked into my chest
Dirty sternum is not sorry   rolls around in a flurry
    untucked cotton
Makes an overcast sky   pure consistent joy   of me

I'll drift a little while   he's already clean
Chosen late for work   easy
Lifting steam   from soon-delivered tea

Trauma poet keeping it light. Serving you queer cripple realness, honey. Big stylistic range ... or just quite confused? **Reanna Valentine** has been published in Ergi Press's *Loki* anthology, *Inksac* by Cephalo Press, Disability Arts Online, and longlisted for the Zealous Amplify creative prize. They starred in the documentary *Collections of Queer Poets*. They host two poetry nights: @QueerThe Mic and @PoetryMeetQT.

The Moment is Perfect, Whole and Complete – L.E. Yates

I glance at my phone.

i know you want it dont pretend you dont

'Thanks, babe,' Mackay calls from under her blanket on the sofa.

'Always busy busy, Meredith,' her sister, Lisa, tosses over her shoulder as I tuck my phone away, pick up the four lipstick-smeared glasses she's scattered around the kitchen and load them into the dishwasher. I still can't get over how strange it is seeing the same thick eyebrows as Mackay's plucked thin, Mackay's strong nose and chin plastered with orangey foundation, and, instead of short black hair, long blonde extensions. I focus instead on the wooden bowl on the worktop and how the evening light falls, yellow and grainy, and fix the image in my head.

It's warm in the house, the dishwasher purring, the clock hands brushing eight, and I can almost ignore the medical tinge that lurks under the savoury smell left from the macrobiotic tofu bowls I made for dinner – but when Lisa loud-whispers to Mackay, 'What's biting her?' I can feel my anger rising. I try to fix an image in my head to centre myself in the moment but fail. I'd promised myself I wasn't going to do this anymore because it was making me feel too awful but I fake-smile at Lisa and take my phone out.

You free tonight? I text back.

I take a deep breath but the reply's almost instant. *meet me in 15 mins usual place*

'Might nip out for a bit,' I say.

Mackay gives me a look that's a little curious but mostly tired. She's always tired.

'Your 9 p.m. dose is there for you.' I nod to the pill caddy on the side.

Lisa pulls a surprised face as she twists her hair up in a knot. 'Oh, I thought we were all going to have an evening together.'

'No big deal.' I smile at her reassuringly. 'I just need a bit of fresh air.' I'm allowed to behave a little erratically from time to time because I'm *bearing up splendidly* and because *it isn't easy, Meredith, being the one to hold it all together* and *they don't know how I'm coping, really, they don't.* People pin me with these phrases like medals. I don't want any of it.

Lisa flew in from LA six weeks ago after several tense phone conversations.

But how long do the doctors say she's got?

She's stopped the chemo but it's not an exact science, Lisa.

Lisa hasn't been back to England for years, certainly not since we'd rented a house by the sea in Norfolk during the pandemic, after Mackay was told the cancer had returned. When I picked Lisa up at the station, I saw her eyeing the car interior before she settled herself gingerly in the passenger seat and it made me notice the fruit pastille wrappers and dusting of sand. With her neat updo, the perfectly coordinated pedal pushers and top, the lilac nail extensions and Gucci luggage there was such an American sheen to her that you wouldn't know she'd grown up in a rough part of Manchester with Mackay.

The shock on Lisa's face as she hugged Mackay for the first time made me see how ill Mackay looks now, her hair thinned like an old lady's until you can see her scalp through the short, lank strands.

No, Lisa, not everyone who has chemotherapy goes completely bald.

As I'm putting on my shoes, Lisa says, 'You're not really going out, are you? You could take a walk any time. We were going to watch *Hustlers* on Netflix.'

There's a moment of sheer, weightless panic as escape slips from my grasp. I can't think what to say.

'Meredith should stay in because I haven't got many evenings left? Is that what you're trying to get at, Lisa?' Mackay's quick black eyes are deep pits in her head, her skin a sallow yellow, but her grin lets me see the woman I fell in love with.

'Jesus Christ, Mackay. I didn't—' Lisa makes an exasperated gesture because it's hard to find the right tone to tell off someone who's dying. This is what Mackay is counting on. She gives me a wink.

I love her so much. I wink back but then the guilt hits me and I feel much worse.

Lisa gives Mackay a look and I can almost hear her talking about me as soon as I've gone. *Such an attitude. What's wrong with her?* But she doesn't understand. I grab my keys.

Mackay gives me another tired smile. 'Thanks for making dinner, love.'

'Of course.' I go to kiss her and try not to mind the chemical smell of her skin. 'Won't be long.'

131

On my way down the hall I stop to grab my jumper from our bedroom. I've slept in my studio upstairs most nights because I've wanted to give Mackay space when she thrashes around in the grip of morphine dreams but we manged to sleep together last night. Both pillows are dented, the bottom sheet rucked on both sides. It won't be long before it will just be me in the king-sized bed. The thought chokes me. Lisa's right. I shouldn't go out tonight. What was I thinking? It was a stupid idea. I hate films like *Hustlers* for their fake feminism, but it'll be easy to hole up on the sofa, Mackay will tuck her feet under my legs, might even stay awake long enough to make it through the first half. Warmth fills me at the thought and the silver-foil-against-fillings mix of excitement and guilt subsides.

But then, as I step into the hall, my gaze catches on the dull metal frame of the light-weight wheelchair, the latest addition to the medical supplies which clutter the house, and something twists inside me. I step back into our bedroom. I start to run through my meditation mantras but I only get from *I am bliss* to *The moment is perfect, whole and complete* before I find myself slamming my fist into the pillows again, then again.

'Meredith?'

I jerk up from the bed, shocked.

Lisa is standing in the doorway, measuring the moment as if she were going to slice it like a butcher. 'Do you know, Meredith? Time is the most precious thing we have. I learnt that the hard way when Howard died.' She comes closer and I can smell her expensive, sickly perfume. 'If I could have bottled every day I had with him, I would have done.'

For a moment another version of Lisa flickers, someone who has loved and experienced loss, someone who might actually have something to share with me, someone I might be close to in the future.

She pushes a diamond bangle up her thin, tanned wrist. 'I can see it's hard to fully appreciate that at your age.'

I push past her and let myself out of the house.

I clear the steps to the street in one bound. It feels good to be out, walking fast away from the house. The small town is quiet, melancholy in the fading light. I'm taking photographs in my head. Trying to fix images is a deliberate practice I've started since Mackay's most recent prognosis. Red light flashes from the kebab shop, yellow shines from the sign over Le Moon Chinese and petrol prices are lit up green at the garage, before the dark blue stripe of the sea. Click.

Being out of the house lets me be more generous. I breathe deeply, try to access compassion. I get it, Lisa, I really do – you're furious. Your only sister's dying. I was furious at the start too but now, Mackay and me, we're just tired. Lisa has some 'live laugh love' thing going on and on the first night insisted on opening a bottle of bad but expensive champagne she'd brought. Mackay can't mix alcohol with the anti-emetic she's taking but she just let her big sister pour her a glass, the bubbles fizzing to flat untouched in front of her, until I took it away.

In the twilight, a bat flickers over the adventure golf. I pass Dunes Amusements, then the helter-skelter down on the prom, flying a St George's Cross.

I check my phone.

don't be late

Excitement leaps inside me.

The smell of frying fat drifts on the summer air as I take the broad tarmacked slope down to the beach. The sun has just set and the sky is like the bottle of coloured sand my gran had on her mantlepiece: dark purple, lavender, pink, orange, peach. The waves are an unreal metallic blue. Click.

I check my phone.

now youre late

With anybody else I would have ignored it. *Sorry*, I text. I realise I'm licking my lips, my lip gloss already gone, a nervous habit.

I hurry past the wooden beach huts, the lit-up steps which lead up the steep, wooded slope back to the town. Abandoned sandcastles are being smoothed by the lick of the tide. The sand nearest the water glints silver in the fading light. It's August but there's no one around.

At the end of the lit promenade, the walkway slopes down onto the sand, banded with stones. Then it gets dark. The shingle crunches beneath my feet. I can smell the wood smoke of a distant fire, the cleanness of salt, the grass releasing its sweetness after the heat of the day.

When I stumble over a lump of flint at the back of the beach someone grabs my arm and I only just stop myself from shouting out. For a moment I'm enveloped by strong arms and a lemony astringent aftershave before I'm set back on my feet again. Jackie must have been tucked against the cliff, waiting, but now I can start to make her shape out of the darkness. She's wearing black jeans and a black T-shirt. As my eyes adjust further, I can see she's smirking.

'You're late. I don't like people being late for me.' She rests her hands lightly on my shoulders like she's steadying me, then she slaps my face and I can feel my lip sting, then the slow, wet seep of blood. 'Get on your knees.'

I get on my knees.

*

It started a month ago. I'd never usually get the bus but I'd been forced to, coming back from a meeting in Hackney about a possible show for my photography, because I'd left the car for Lisa. She'd insisted on driving Mackay to Holkham Beach, which she'd read about online, even though I'd told her Mackay wouldn't be able to manage the walk from the carpark to the dunes.

It was hot on the bus and the squawking of panda-eyed teenagers and inane chat of pensioners meant I was already waiting by the front door when we finally lurched up to the stop on Church Street.

'Oi, you dropped this.'

The bus driver's rough tone made me blanch. 'Oh, sorry, I don't think I ... I think you've made a mistake ...'

Two teenagers wriggled past me but the bus driver met my gaze, unblinking. 'Don't think I have.' She held out an old ticket.

I'd noticed the driver when I got on and tried to give her a comradely you're-gay-I'm-gay nod as she punched my ticket. She was tall and broad shouldered, a little bit younger than me, maybe mid-twenties, with short, curly black hair. She seemed to disdain the military pretension of her bus driver's uniform – she wore the short-sleeved shirt with red epaulettes untucked, the badge crooked.

Her small black eyes held mine with a trace of amusement as I took the ticket from her. She was handsome, in a rough, local way. I don't know how else to describe it. You don't really see people like her in London.

Once I'd stepped off the bus, I turned the shiny paper over. On it she'd written, *call 07783428196 if you want to do more than just stare at me.*

I blushed crimson and crumpled her note up as the bus spurted off down the street.

I come hard on my hands and knees, my breathing ragged, the pebbles shifting awkwardly beneath me. She pulls her fingers out of my cunt and wipes them across my face.

'What do you say?'

'Thank you?'

She reaches out a hand to yank me up.

There's no moon tonight and the stars are tiny white flecks in ink. We slog back over the shingle in the darkness, not touching, until we reach the concrete slipway where the lights begin.

Jackie turns me to her, more gently this time, and I try not to flinch. 'Went hard on you, didn't I?' She gives my face another glance. 'Can't let you walk through town like this.'

I bring my hand up to my lip and it comes away smeared brown in the orangey light.

'How far away do you live?'

'Not far,' I say but the thought of going home – the too-hot house, Mackay and Lisa curled up in front of the television – is stifling.

'Mine's just round the corner.'

At first I'm not sure what she's offering but when she carries straight on at the top of the slope, where I would have turned right, it's easy just to follow her. The streets off the prom are a brightly lit shock.

'Did you see that sign about the Cromer Bagots?'

'What?' Jackie looks at me with suspicion in her sloe eyes.

'They're the goats that live on the cliffs but they sound

like some sort of posh family. "Oh, do you know the Cromer Bagots?"' I'm babbling, still high from what we've done.

'What are you on about?' She gives my hair an amused ruffle.

I'm struck by a pang at how far apart we feel then. Mackay would have laughed.

She climbs the stone steps of one of the four-storey, crumbling red-brick terraces. A dismal run of buzzers signals its division into flats. Inside, the hall smells of gas. As I follow her up the grubby stair carpet, past a landing with two flimsy doors, my uneasiness increases. Going home with her is a whole new betrayal.

Her flat has that stale-teacake-charity-shop whiff and there's no real sign that anyone lives there beyond the pristine white trainers under the radiator in the living room and a scatter of rolling papers and tobacco on an ugly, glass-topped coffee table. The loneliness of the room overwhelms me. I shouldn't have come.

'Sit. There.' She points to a black fake-leather sofa. She disappears then kneels down in front of me and looks up into my face to dab at my lip with some bunched-up toilet roll.

The way her hair curls on her neck as she's so tenderly undoing what she's done fills me with that welling feeling that can come after fucking, but what undoes me is how well she looks, her glossy hair, the freckles over her nose, the sleek animal strength that I no longer take for granted in the bodies I touch. For a flash I hate her and her good health as purely as I've ever hated anyone. It takes all of my energy to contain this so it doesn't burst out in words.

Jackie stands up, chucks the waded toilet paper down,

then tugs open the top button of her jeans. 'Fancy another go?'

I get on my knees again.

I walk home, trying not to think about what I've just done. The memory of Mackay winking at me earlier squeezes at my heart. When I turn onto our street I stop in an orange patch of streetlight to read the message Jackie has just sent. *your the hottest fuck.*

Lisa's curled up on the sofa like a smug Cheshire Cat when I get in.

'You took your time.' Lisa's accent sounds suddenly northern, the edge in her voice displacing that annoying American twang.

I'm about to say, 'Why does it matter?' before fear darts through me like a thousand silver fish. 'Is Mackay all right?'

'Mackay? Yeah, she's fine. Just gone to bed.'

I'm heading into the kitchen to make a green tea when Lisa says, 'You might want to delete WhatsApp off your laptop.'

'What?' I stop still in the doorway.

But Lisa's looking down at the stick she's buffing her nails with. 'It updated, then that last message you got popped up on screen while we were watching the end of the film.'

A cold horror fills me. When she looks up she can see the question forming inside me because she says, 'Mackay didn't see it. She was asleep.'

Lisa's watching, waiting to see what I'm going to say. All the way through I've told myself that Mackay would understand if I told her, that sexual jealousy never felt like a big deal between us, that I just didn't want to burden her while she had so much to contend with, but now this feels flimsy. I think I'm going to be sick.

Lisa stares at me. I hold my breath, wait for the axe to fall, for her to say, 'You need to tell Mackay or I already have,' but she has a curious expression on her face and instead she says, 'You know, when Howard was ill, I used to drive to the office on the days I was still working. I'd always take my time, smell the flowers, get a coffee on Wilshire, because being out of the house felt like a treat, then every Friday evening when it got to 6.30 and the office emptied out, I'd go into Meeting Room 3 and fuck the senior vice president of marketing.'

She's looking at me, and I can feel surprise spreading across my face.

'I did that for the whole three months. I didn't even fancy the guy that much. I think he liked me because he asked me to go for dinner with him a couple of months after Howard's funeral. Joe Romano, he was called. Bristles like a warthog.' She gives the nail of her little finger a final buff. 'I told him I wasn't interested.'

'Right,' I say. 'Yes.'

'I get it, Meredith. You just want to feel in touch with the living.' When our eyes meet, her brown gaze is steady and she sees me, really sees me. I go to smile but then her face shuts up, foundation and blusher hardening like a mask. 'I'd delete WhatsApp desktop, though, if I were you.'

In the bedroom, Mackay's lying on her back, eyes closed, a line of spit coming from the corner of her mouth. Her breathing's rough as tearing paper. She's only forty-three but she doesn't look it now. This isn't an image I want to keep in my head. I sit on the edge of the bed gently so I don't wake her.

I take Mackay's hand. 'I love you so much.' And I know

as I say it that this is true whether I'm sitting next to her now or on my hands and knees on the beach.

I look at her sunken cheeks, the jagged line of her profile, and the pain is so great that I think I won't survive her death when it comes but then I know that I will and that's when I start to cry.

L.E. Yates was born in Manchester in 1981 but now lives in east London. She's interested in the imaginative loopholes fiction creates in everyday life. She has been awarded Arts Council England funding and her writing has appeared in anthologies from *Parenthesis* to *Dead Languages*. Her short story, 'Sunblock', won the Costa Short Story Award in 2021.

Words of One Syllable – V.G. Lee

Every three months or so I come into London for a dental appointment – ongoing problem with a wisdom tooth – and the surgery is only walking distance from Hilary's mother's flat. Next to the tube station is a Sainsbury's where I buy chocolate eclairs for us both.

On my last visit, Carol, the day carer met me at the front door. 'Don't expect too much. Barbara's having a bad day.'

I followed her into the living room where Barbara was tucked into a corner of the sofa. A crocheted blanket lay across her knees.

'Cakes', I said, holding up the box.

Slowly she turned her head to look at me but there was no welcoming smile.

I made tea and put the eclairs on plates. 'And, how are you?' I asked, sinking down into one of the two armchairs.

'Not bad. OK.'

'Seen the boys?' (The boys and girls – Barbara's children and grandchildren – are now aged between thirty and sixty.)

'I don't think so.'

From the kitchen the carer called out, 'Of course you've seen your sons. They pop in every day.'

Finally, Barbara smiled with a hint of cheekiness, as if she'd played a joke on us by pretending to forget.

Usually if I prompt her with questions about film stars from the nineteen-forties and fifties, I can get a lively conversation going. Barbara's likes and dislikes are emphatic: she adored Spencer Tracy and Clark Gable, found Cary Grant *smarmy*, didn't care tuppence for Gregory Peck. But for the first time ever she confined her answers to words of one syllable or silence. I found myself droning on about black spot on my roses and the holiday in Malta Hilary and I might or might not take later in the year. However, when she'd finished the eclair, she lowered the plate to her lap and with genuine delight exclaimed 'Delicious!' That one relatively complicated word gave me hope that the Barbara I knew and cared about was still functioning in whatever world she'd withdrawn into.

Today, three months later, Barbara's *boys* are assembled in her living room; Hilary is out in the kitchen making tea.

'Can I help?' I ask.

She shakes her head, lays the palm of her hand on her breastbone.

'I'm sorry,' I say. 'I know how hard this must be for you.'

She shrugs. I return to my chair at the back of the room.

Watching Hilary and her brothers, listening to their conversations, I'm constantly reminded of scenes from Francis Ford Coppola's film *The Godfather* – that emphasis on family and hierarchy. There is no doubt that Barbara is – was – a matriarch: the mother who not only ruled and dominated, but loved her family almost beyond reason.

However reluctant they might sometimes feel as they twist and turn to prise her hook from their hearts, none can help but return her love. She is the best mother. They are the best children. And in truth I don't disagree.

I am the friend of thirty years – female equivalent of the character Tom Hagen, *consigliere* to the film's Corleone family. I'm reliable, I make them laugh, for the most part they trust me, but sometimes I think I could just as easily be disposed of!

The television is switched on but with the sound barely audible. The door to the flat's Juliet balcony stands open in an effort to clear the fug of youngest son Andrew's cigarettes. Sitting around the coffee table these elderly children play cards. They talk, smoke and later as the afternoon closes in, drink wine and beer. Andrew produces sausage sandwiches for all and now there's a tomato ketchup stain on the beige sofa. Sunk deep in an armchair, Simon, the oldest looks up from his phone as if he's about to make some critical comment then thinks better of it. Between this room and the kitchen, James, the middle son drifts. He has gained a little weight recently but I know he'll lose it once this is over.

In Barbara's bedroom, a narrow bed has replaced her double divan. There are rails on each side to prevent her from falling out. A dark blue protective sheet covers the mattress – an unintentional insult to this woman who loved her pastel patterned duvet sets. Head tucked into her shoulders, shoulders tense against a bank of pillows, Barbara makes me think of a broken bird.

'Come closer,' Hilary instructs. 'Mum can't see you properly.'

I take a step towards the bed and Barbara's eyes focus on my face.

'Hello Julia,' she whispers.

'Hello.' I feel inordinately pleased that she's recognised me. And then her gaze dulls and I'm forgotten.

It is hard to believe that Barbara is in her nineties. Her skin remains unlined. Her bare feet are surprisingly slim and youthful. If all I could see were those feet, toes flexing on a patch of hot summer grass, I'd assume that they belonged to a woman in early middle-age, with a husband who loves her but has rarely broken through his wife's deep reserve. Definitely she would be a mother – three boys, one girl – living in a bright, well-kept house in the suburbs. Barbara would drive a car and wash her own windows. In early summer she'd plant out geraniums, fuchsia, salvia, lobelia and alyssum. She would take pride in her roses. Yes, this would be Barbara as I first knew her, before the grandchildren, before the great grandchild.

I was twenty-nine when I persuaded my husband to let me go to Art College as a mature student. At that time, I had only the vaguest knowledge of women's rights and even if they'd been spelt out to me, I wouldn't have summoned up the courage to assert them. Instead, I wheedled and simpered, used my feminine wiles as I'd watched my own mother do with my father. During my second week at college I noticed Hilary. She was always at the centre of a group of the popular students; always with something to say that they wanted to listen to. Her smile was amazing. It lit up an otherwise sallow face. One evening in a pub when I should have been on a train heading homewards, she told me she was a lesbian. Having never met a lesbian before, I was fascinated.

We began a clandestine affair which lasted five years. What an old-fashioned word *clandestine* seems to be, but it was an old-fashioned affair. We took foolish risks; there were rows and reconciliations, jealousy on both sides, difficult telephone conversations while my unsuspecting husband watched television in the next room. Somehow, we were never discovered.

On the day I told Hilary that I'd decided to leave my marriage, our affair finished. I'd assumed she'd be over-joyed. On so many occasions she'd begged me to pack my bags and move in with her. The look of horrified shock on her face was a blow to my heart. From believing I was the love of someone's life, in a matter of minutes I'd become a responsibility. Worse; a liability.

'But are you sure?' she'd stammered. 'Where will you live?'

I'm glad I didn't say, 'With you.'

I'm glad I said, 'Oh, I'll sort myself out,' as if our affair had nothing to do with my decision.

After a while I found myself able to understand and even sympathise. Hilary dreaded her mother's disapproval. An affair Barbara might have accepted, but not an affair with a woman. She would have seen me as a threat to her own relationship with her daughter. That was an upsetting period in my life. Hilary and I could have gone our separate ways, but I hung on. I still hold the hurt and no doubt Hilary still holds the guilt. It took years but we hammered out a friendship. We are the best of friends.

And Barbara? Initially I was apprehensive at the thought of the two of us finally coming face to face. Even during the affair, she was constantly telephoning Hilary, always breaking into the limited time the two of us were able to spend together. Following her calls, Hilary would be distracted no matter how hard she tried to hide it.

'Bloody mother. Bloody Barbara. Well, perhaps I should pop in later. The boys are out at a football match.'

'But isn't your father with her?'

'He'll be glued to the television.'

Hilary spent a further two years putting out the forest fire of our relationship. Only when she felt the last spark was extinguished did she introduce me to Barbara. I expected to dislike her on sight. I remember I was waiting with Hilary outside a hair salon in West Ruislip. By then I fully appreciated that if I had any chance of maintaining a friendship with her daughter, I had to make the right impression, appear low-key, vulnerable, passive.

'I'm nervous,' I said.

'Me too.' From the butt of her cigarette, Hilary lit another.

Finally, Barbara emerged from the salon: a small, compact woman wearing an unremarkable skirt and twin-set and clutching a mushroom-coloured handbag. The only touch of colour was a mauve chiffon scarf draped around her neck.

'This is my friend, Julia,' Hilary said.

Barbara smiled at me. 'Hilary's told me so much about you. All good.'

'That's a relief,' I said.

'Mum's a martyr to her hair,' Hilary was grinning. 'It's a family joke that she's visited every hairdresser in West London.'

'Well it looks lovely,' I said.

'Do you think so?' Barbara touched her hair tentatively. In those days it was brown with only a few threads of grey. 'I think I'm pleased.'

'You should be!' I meant it. Her hair was so thick and shiny. 'The first hint of rain and mine becomes frizzy.'

Suddenly I had her full attention, 'Not frizz, dear. Curls. I've always wanted curls.'

There and then, something in me – let me claim it as what was left of my heart – warmed to her.

Barbara's body is cramped into the top half of the bed. The nurse has dressed her in fresh pyjamas: patterned trousers with a matching top. Barbara would have approved of the choice. But she wouldn't be pleased with her hair. In her frustration she has tugged the short white layers into an unflattering Goth peak above her forehead.

Earlier the eldest son remarked, 'Mum looks very well.'

That must have been wishful thinking because Barbara looks far from well. But nor does she look physically ill. Imagine a wild animal caught in a trap; gaze desperately roaming above our heads as if we too are part of the plan to hold her captive, which of course we are. As Barbara pushes against the pillows, the expression on her face is of angry determination. With surprising strength, her legs kick out over the bed rails.

One of the visiting nurses has shown Hilary how to lift a patient and now she manoeuvres her mother's body so Barbara lies facing upwards. We both return her legs to the safety of the bed and slide cushions beneath her knees. Barbara has been unravelled, but it brings her no relief.

'Please,' she cries out again and again.

Is she pleading for a miracle, a turning back of the clock?

Where do these lived-in faces come from? Take them away and let me see my children.

I'm reminded of a time – not so many years ago – when she was still capable of catching a train from Waterloo to visit Hilary at her house on the south coast. It was winter and very cold. There was some weather-related reason for the train to be delayed and then the passengers had to change to a bus replacement for the last section of the journey. In driving snow, Hilary drove down to the train station, leaving me in her living room watching an old episode of *Columbo*. I remember the front door flying open as Hilary erupted into the room. Behind her came Barbara, smart in a camel-coloured winter coat and knee-high leather boots. Both were laughing, pleased as Punch to be in each other's company. I didn't mind. I was far too fond of both women to be jealous.

'Warmth!' Barbara shouted, heading for the radiator. 'I was frozen on the bus.'

While Hilary made hot drinks, Barbara regaled us with stories: the kind man at Waterloo Station who had lifted her up from the platform to the train. 'The gap was huge. If he hadn't helped, I could have slipped under the carriage and been killed!' Of the female passenger who announced as the snow shower became a blizzard, 'We're all going to die!' The whole carriage erupted into laughter and then grew quiet as they considered the very real possibility. 'The train lost power and the lights went off, you see,' Barbara explained. 'But I'm here now.'

All the Marie Curie nurses in attendance have been stunned by the love and concern shown by Barbara's family.

Yesterday everyone was close to tears but today, Simon – the most vulnerable, or so it seems to me – sets aside his mobile phone and says, 'We're a reserved bunch. Personally, I'm turned off by extravagant displays of emotion.' He falls silent.

We wait as he assembles more words.

'But I seem to recall many years ago,' Simon frowns in an effort to remember, 'Hilary was still in the pram or stroller – whatever it was. We turned into this dark alley. I was frightened. Mum said, "Simon, hold my hand." And I did. The fear disappeared. Holding her hand made me feel safe.'

'You're imagining it,' James says. 'Why would mum take you both down a dark alley?'

'It was a cut-through between the streets. As we came out, she said, "Phew!" As if she was relieved.'

'Hmm.' James raises an unimpressed eyebrow.

'Honestly James, it does exist. Drove around the area yesterday and there it was: a passage between two houses. I might go back and take a photo. Nothing sentimental.' Embarrassed, he returns to his phone.

Hilary clears the mugs, glasses and ashtrays off the coffee table so they can play cards again later. One of the grandsons arrives with Kate, another daughter-in-law. They all spend time with Barbara. Kate massages her chilly feet. 'Perhaps she's cold,' Hilary suggests, covering Barbara with a blanket, but immediately she kicks the blanket off.

Outside it's begun to rain. Only five o'clock in the afternoon but already it's growing dark. One of the nurses tells us not to attempt giving the patient water with the plastic invalid cup. She increases the dose of morphine to control Barbara's terminal agitation. Someone else carries an armchair into the bedroom. A grandchild hovers in the doorway, watching.

In the hall I fish my jacket out of the pile of all their jackets and coats.

Hilary turns to me. 'Can't you stay a little longer? You always cheer us up.'

'Work tomorrow,' I say. As much as I love them . . . as the outsider, the *consigliere* – it is time to leave.

'So, when will we see you again? No, don't answer that. Oh god.' She squeezes my arm. 'Well, safe journey home.'

'Thank you.'

From the living room comes a chorus, 'Safe journey home, Julia.'

It is only on the train heading back into central London that I find myself picking over Hilary's final brief sentences; thinking with a degree of pain, if she'd only used the word 'me' instead of 'us', 'I' instead of 'we'. Now this thought, like a revelation, is in my head, I fear I'll always be listening out for that discrepancy between what I hear and what I want to hear and eventually the weight of those single syllables will become unbearable.

V.G. Lee is the author of five novels and two collections of short stories. In 2012 Lee was nominated for a Stonewall Award for writing. Her most recent novel, *Mr Oliver's Object of Desire* was runner-up for the 2017 YLVA Publishing Literary Prize for Fiction. In 2022 she was longlisted for the BBC's National Short Story Award.

That's the Part I Love Most –
Dale Booton

when you stay   and after
the sheets remain unchanged for days   made
and unmade by the rushing tenure
of your husk

i wake up wanting to touch you   reach
into the besideme space filled
with absence   the hollowness
like a blanket

drag it over me   myself
in the memory of your body   there
imagine us in the years
to come

once staying became stayed
and the flesh once smooth has creased
like sheets   washed and re-washed
in your scent

Dale Booton (he/him) is a queer poet from Birmingham. His poetry has been published in various places, such as Verve, Young Poets Network, *Queerlings*, *The North*, Muswell Press, and Magma.His debut pamphlet *Walking Contagions* is out with Polari Press. Twitter: @BootsPoetry

Two Butches Walk into a Bra Shop – Max Hartley

'I don't think that's gonna work,' said Meg, pointing at the bra in Ri's hands. 'Too many hooks at the back.'

'But it's red. I thought that was supposed to be hot?' Ri replied, immediately replacing it on the rail.

'It's hot until it's impossible to undo it, and then she'll have to take over. That's not hot.'

Meg ruffled her spiky, salt-and-pepper hair while she mused.

'What about this?' she said, picking up an ashy blue bralette with some sort of netting in place of cups.

'Maybe,' Ri said. 'But Jamie's kind of self-conscious about her boobs.'

As her mouth rounded into the 'oo' sound of boobs, she caught the eye of a frowning woman opposite her.

'Do you ever get the feeling,' Ri said, turning her whole body towards Meg and speaking from the side of her mouth, 'that when you go out as a pair of queers, people can suddenly read you better than when you're on your own?'

'If you mean that woman over there, she definitely thinks

we're trans women invading her personal space in a public shopping centre.'

'Oh,' said Ri. 'There I was thinking she didn't like lesbians.'

'No babe, you've got it all wrong. Women who hate trans women absolutely love lesbians. Especially butch lesbians.'

'Especially in toilets and changing rooms,' Ri added.

'Gives them a chance to strike up a friendly conversation about the fact that we must be lost.'

They laughed under their breath until Ri saw that Meg was struggling to stay quiet, her face turning from pale to pink to red, and then she burst into a loud cackle. Ri groaned as the woman approached a shop assistant, attempting to point at the two of them without turning around.

'For fuck's sake,' said Meg.

Ri began fingering black negligees in a way that she hoped looked natural and carefree, while Meg muttered increasingly frantically next to her.

'She's coming over she's coming over – mate, she's coming over she's—'

'Hi there,' said a youngish woman, blonde hair tucked behind her ears to show off a couple of gold hoops. 'Can I help you with something?'

Ri noticed, as she always did, that the assistant had deliberately avoided calling them 'guys' or 'ladies', the word that was thrown around about three times a sentence for those who could confidently be labelled as ladies. Still, it was better than when people took a punt one way and then saw a new detail – a necklace? Thick eyebrows? The slight press of breasts against a shirt? – that made them reconsider and go into a tailspin, apologies dripping from their mouths like hot fat.

'We're fine, thanks,' Ri said. She fiddled at the zip of her hoodie with clammy fingers.

'Great,' the assistant smiled. Her name badge said she was called Leanne. Ri felt a twinge of guilt that Leanne had been put in this position because of her. Except, she corrected herself, it wasn't because of her. 'I'm really sorry but, um, the lady who was at the till just now felt uncomfortable.'

'Is that why she was buying a new bra?' Meg asked, giving Leanne a nudge with her elbow.

Leanne forced a laugh that ended up sounding more like a shriek.

'It's just . . . the lady felt that she couldn't be here at the same time.'

'And the lady didn't want to tell us herself?' Meg said, putting her thumbs into her belt loops. 'Well, let's go and be ladies elsewhere, Ri. Where our ladylike cash is more appreciated.'

Meg sauntered out of the shop and Ri followed, giving Leanne an apologetic grimace over her shoulder.

'This is why I only do online shopping,' Ri said, as they collected themselves on a bench outside Boots. 'It's always excruciating one way or another.'

'Fuck that,' Meg said. 'I'm not waiting days to try on horrendous clothes that don't fit and then having to go to the post office *at lunchtime* to return them. I'd rather go back to giving blow jobs.'

Ri raised her chin slightly in response.

'Not that there's anything wrong with giving blow jobs,' Meg added, as a splotch of pink arrived at her cheekbones.

'Shall we try M&S?'

'I thought Jamie wanted something spicy?'

'I actually don't know what she wants at all. I'm going out on a limb here.'

'So it's a gift for you,' Meg said, pressing her palms against her thighs as she stood up. 'And your dream is to see your girlfriend in a beige T-shirt bra. You make absolutely no sense to me.'

*

Ri was watchful as they made their way through the shopping centre. Being with Meg when they were in private felt like taking her bra off after a long day, sweet relief. In public, it felt like wearing a bra with a bit of loose underwire that's stabbing you repeatedly in the ribs. While Ri would look down if they were glared at, Meg stared back even harder. If somebody muttered that they were dykes, Meg would yell back that their mum was too. But today it was quiet, blazing sun keeping most people out in flagged beer gardens and parks turned dusty from weeks of heat.

When they reached the lingerie section, Meg marched towards the underwear, looking jubilant. She rifled through the bras like she was shuffling a deck of cards, rapid and expert.

'Hmph,' she said finally, looking disappointed. 'They're actually quite nice.'

'What's your favourite?'

'For me or for Rina?'

'For you. Or, both, I guess.'

'Well, I gave up trying to hide my boobs a long time ago,' Meg said, plucking out a plain black underwire bra. 'Because they're fucking huge. I'd say, "in case you hadn't noticed" but obviously you have noticed.'

'They are pretty big.'

'They're not "pretty big",' she said dismissively. 'They're an H cup.'

'Would you ever get a reduction? Or,' Ri hesitated. 'Get rid of them?'

'With all the money I've got?'

'If it was free, would you?'

'Hm. Ideal for me would be not having them except when I was having sex. Rina can't get enough of them.'

'Oh,' Ri said. 'I didn't know you liked that.'

'I like seeing her turned on,' Meg shrugged. 'I don't think about it much more than that.'

They wandered past more plain bras and sensible briefs with bows on the front.

'Something on your mind?' Meg said. 'Other than my tits?'

Ri gave her a shove.

'I'm just sick of mine. Wish I could donate them to someone who'd appreciate them.'

'Surely Jamie appreciates them.'

'Yeah,' Ri said. 'But I don't like them being appreciated.'

'Oh,' said Meg. 'That hasn't changed?'

'Nope.'

'Are you saying that you're . . .?'

They let the word hang between them in the air, unspoken but solid.

'I have no idea,' Ri said.

'Is it something you've chatted about with Jamie? How's this, by the way?' Meg held up a mint-green padded bra and matching pants.

'That's the best thing we've seen, isn't it?'

'Yup. Now can we go for a pint?'

*

'So,' Meg said as they collapsed down at their usual spot away from the toilets, jukebox, smoking area, and other people. 'You're trans.'

'Let's . . . not go that far,' Ri said, glancing around them. 'It's hard to know if disliking a body part is a trans thing or a woman thing, isn't it?'

'Because we're brought up to dislike our bodies.'

'Yeah. So I guess the question is more about *why* I dislike them so much.'

'Your boobs.'

Ri nodded, jaw set.

'Why do you dislike them?'

'Dunno.'

'OK. I think you do.'

Ri sighed. Meg was probably right. But sometimes she wished Meg would be more gentle with her. She pushed her glasses back up her nose and took a breath.

'How's life now you've moved in with Rina, anyway?' Ri asked.

'Bliss.'

'Yeah?'

'Yep. Nobody in the kitchen, nobody in the bathroom, nobody watching TV. No more buses across town. Loads more sex.'

'Happy for you.'

'You get so uptight whenever I talk about shagging.'

'I do not.'

Meg arched an eyebrow.

'You know I thought you were great in bed.'

'Meg!'

'What!' Meg said, hands up. 'Just trying to reassure you.'

'I don't nee—'

'How's sex with Jamie?'

Ri puffed a breath out of her nose.

'Really good, thanks.'

'What's your favourite bit?'

'Coming?'

Meg rolled her eyes.

'You know what I mean.'

Ri took a swig of her pint and felt bubbles hit the roof of her mouth, tiny explosions that made her shoulders tense.

'Well . . . I like it when she goes down on me but touches herself at the same time. And when she tops.'

'So you're really embracing life as a pillow princess. Or prince.'

'Rina never tops you?'

'She does,' Meg said, picking up her pint and then replacing it on the table. 'But only when I tell her to.'

'You're really embracing life as a dom, then.'

They locked eyes for a second and something dangerous passed between them.

'Couldn't have done it without you.'

Ri scoffed, thinking it might dispel the lightning bolts threatening to crack above them.

'I hope Jamie likes this stuff, after all this,' she said.

'She will,' Meg said, folding her empty crisp packet into a neat triangle. Her fingers were stubby but dextrous. 'She knows you wear the same bra every day, so it's obvious you tried.'

*

At home, Jamie was taking a bath. She'd filled it with menthol-scented bubble bath and run the water so hot that the tiles were dripping with condensation. The only part of her body that had crested the surface of the water was her penis, the soft nub of it haloed by suds. And her nipples, deep red and oblong like pomegranate seeds in their cream casing.

'Hey babe,' Ri said, flapping her way through dense clouds of steam. 'How was your birthday eve?'

Jamie stuck out her tongue to mime vomiting.

'Remind me to book off the whole week next year,' she said.

'Was lunch OK?'

'Meh. I stuck around with Harvey and Mo.'

'They're the sweet ones?' Ri said.

Jamie had coated herself in oil that smelled like vanilla and musk. When she turned to face Ri, her face shimmered like the sea on a clear night, the peaks and dips of it catching in the candlelight.

'Yep. Two out of twenty. I have a theory that they don't mind that I'm queer because I, too, have a teenager's job when I'm in my thirties.'

'What makes something a teenager's job?' Ri asked.

'The fact that everybody else who works there is a teenager.'

'You know I'll help you look for other stuff,' said Ri. She reached out to touch Jamie's hair but pulled back when she saw the look of horror on her face – she'd smoothed it out with scoops of buttery conditioner. 'You're the one with the degree, after all.'

'Yeah,' Jamie laughed. 'And you're the one that's cis. Swings and roundabouts.'

'About that,' Ri said, stripping off. 'I think ... maybe I'm not?'

'Oh,' Jamie said, an uphill lilt in her voice.

It was how she sounded when she received unexpected pleasant news. *They accidentally gave us two bottles of red wine in the Tesco delivery. I don't start work until eleven tomorrow. Your legs look incredible in those jeans.* Ri lowered herself into the bath behind Jamie, feeling the water lapping over her thighs and up to her vulva.

'What made you realise?' Jamie said. 'Don't worry, it's not going to overflow.'

'Might do once my boobs are in,' said Ri, gently placing them into the water. 'It was that book you gave me. *The Breast.*'

Jamie threw her head back to laugh, her throat juddering with the force of it.

'"Philip Roth made me trans,"' Jamie said, pretending to type. 'Bet you could get fifty quid for that.'

'It just got me thinking,' Ri mumbled.

'As in, "What if, instead of turning into a breast, I could have no breasts at all?"'

'I know you're joking, but ...'

'This is,' Jamie said, reaching behind her to take Ri's hands. 'Incredible.'

'Is it?'

'Yes,' Jamie said. 'The fact that this is what cracked your egg makes me love you even more.'

Ri felt herself smile, uncoupled her hands from Jamie's so she could hold her around the waist.

'I'm glad you're happy about it,' she said. 'It's not 100% certain, obviously.'

'Obviously,' Jamie said. 'Never heard that one before.'

Ri placed her cheek on Jamie's shoulder, feeling stung. They sat quietly, listening to the offbeat drip of the tap into the bath, how it echoed off the wet walls.

'I got your present today,' she said.

'When you were out with Meg?'

'Yeah.'

'Shopping for your partner with your ex? A classic of the genre.'

'Meg isn't my ex,' Ri trilled.

'Does Meg know that?'

'Fuck off.'

'I'll let that slide because I'm intrigued about the gift,' Jamie said.

'A day early?'

'It's half eleven.'

'Well, you'll have to get out of the bath first. It can't get wet.'

Afterwards, Ri lay on their bed in a waffle dressing gown, watching Jamie towel off. She rubbed baby oil into her hands, warming it between them, then palmed her body in wide circles. Ri loved how Jamie's flesh stretched and folded, the creases that deepened and disappeared like it was dough being expertly kneaded.

'You smell amazing,' Ri said.

'My mum used to do this after every shower,' Jamie said. 'Reminds me of her.'

As Jamie approached her, one knee at either side of her thighs, Ri noticed tiny discs of oil on the surface of her skin.

'You're like a dolphin,' Ri said, rubbing Jamie's slick stomach with her thumbs. 'So shiny.'

'I aim to please.'

Jamie waited while Ri rubbed the rest of the oil in, feeling Ri's palms against her back and buttocks, then her fingers in the space between them.

'Does that feel good?' Ri asked. She kept her left hand clamped on Jamie's hip, holding her in place.

'It'd feel even better after a present,' Jamie smiled.

Ri let her skull fall back on the headboard.

'Ow,' she said. 'Fine. Off you get.'

She ran downstairs, feeling the carpet between her toes as she landed. The only thing she could find to wrap the underwear in was some tissue paper Jamie had left over from Christmas. It was vaguely festive looking, but Jamie wasn't fussy about those things.

Meg had always pulled her up on the tiniest details. Leaving the price sticker on the back of birthday cards. Forgetting the hazelnut shot in her coffee. Doing the flicky thing with her tongue too fast or too slow.

'If you don't like it, I've got the gift receipt,' Ri said, placing the package on Jamie's lap.

Jamie peeled back each layer of tissue paper so cautiously it seemed like she was scared to find out what was inside. Eventually, she unfolded the underwear, unravelling the straps that Ri had tangled up.

'This is very pretty,' she said, holding it to the light.

'Yeah?' Ri said, approaching the bed.

'I should go and put it on, shouldn't I?' she laughed. 'Sorry.'

'If you want to,' Ri grinned. 'Or I can just close my eyes.'

'Yes,' Jamie said. 'Imagine you haven't just seen me naked and that I've gone from fully clothed to wearing lingerie.'

Ri scrunched her eyes shut. Behind her eyelids she could see spreadsheets, Jamie in the bath, Rina fucking Meg.

'You can open your eyes now.'

'Wow,' Ri breathed.

'Thanks,' Jamie said, chin ducked. 'Should I do a twirl?'

Ri nodded, and Jamie turned on the spot, arms over her head like a ballerina. The material was gauzy enough that Ri could make out Jamie's nipples and pubic hair, both hazily pressing against their constraints. They kissed hard, Ri opening her mouth to let Jamie's tongue go deeper, only drawing back when their teeth clashed.

'Turn over,' Jamie muttered, taking Ri by the hips.

Jamie had always overwhelmed Ri, from the very start. From their first date which had begun at a chain Italian restaurant, the two of them tearing into a giant garlic pizza, Ri marvelling at Jamie folding her slices in half and devouring them in four bites, her lips glazed with oil. The two of them bonding over their parents' 'I don't mind it's just that–' reactions to them coming out, to the damage that had done, slow-motion car crash style, over the years. The tipsy walk back to Ri's flat, now their flat, arms around each other's waists, hoping that even with hangovers they'd still feel love-drunk in the morning. How Jamie had been timid, at first, unsure of herself, how Ri had found herself begging and then got what she'd asked for, to be overcome. Which was where she found herself now, forehead against her forearms, Jamie's stomach against her back, the skin of them sticking, Jamie asking her, as always, if she liked it. Which she always did.

Afterwards, they rolled away from one another to scroll. Twitter for Jamie; Facebook for Ri. That's how you could tell there was an age gap, Jamie said.

A WhatsApp from Meg:

Did she like it??

   Yeah I think so

Did you bother asking????

'Babe,' Ri said, rolling her head against her shoulder. 'You did like the present, right?'

'Sure,' Jamie shrugged, smiling.

'Sure?'

'Yeah. Sure.'

Ri locked her phone and let it drop into her lap.

'Why do I not feel convinced?'

'Well,' Jamie said. 'The reason I only have sports bras is because I like them the most.'

'Oh,' Ri frowned. 'It's not that lingerie's too expensive?'

'Nope.'

'Oh.'

'Maybe next time you can take me shopping instead,' Jamie said to her phone.

'Noted.'

'Or we could go to Gino's?'

Gino's, where Meg had spent the full two-hour meal with her hand pressed between Ri's legs. Ri felt her stomach flip.

'Nah. Let's try the new Thai place in town.'

Max Hartley is originally from Burnley, now based in north London. By day, they work as a copywriter for a children's charity. By night, they eat a lot of chocolate digestives and write about queer people, queer relationships, and, sometimes, themselves. Most recently, their story The Yellow Luminescence was named a Top 60 entry to the BBC's National Short Story Award, and was published by clavmag.

Half of This, Half of That – Divin Ishimwe

It is incredible to be somewhat unique in a culture where everything seems to follow a strict set of rules and patterns. However, being different comes with a very heavy burden. Especially when you feel like you have to constantly explain yourself and fight the whole world. It is exhausting, and being different can easily become a nightmare we would never wish to find ourselves in.

I am a young African queer artist nerd, from Burundi. But I'm not your typical, 'flawless' queer. I don't like clubs and dancing. I don't drink alcohol and I am a Christian. I am too queer for my society yet not queer enough for the LGBTQ+ community, which is sometimes amusing, and sometimes troubling.

I grew up in a very religious family within an extremely conservative society which considers queer people a threat to the whole country. When I was kid, my family always said to me, 'Be a man.' Whenever they questioned my choices, that is what they would say, as though they were worried that I was not man enough. They never appreciated that I was drawn to books, soft music, theatre or nature. I would constantly be compared to my cousins who were more athletic and played basketball for their high schools. They seemed to be the kind of sons my family wished for.

When I would walk down my neighbourhood, other boys would point fingers at me and shout 'Look at this gay!' because I wasn't playing football with them in the afternoon or wouldn't sit with them on the side of the streets in the evenings. Many times, I would hold back my tears so that I would not break down in front of them. Then, I would rush home, run to my room, close the door behind me and weep. I would ask God why he made me the way he did. What did I do to deserve such resentment? I could not fight back then. I was not physically or emotionally strong enough. I was just a kid who had to grow up fast in order to survive.

During my free time, I would go to Google and type 'queer black men' because I knew that my current environment would never accept or tolerate the person I was growing to be. I had to seek out my own community. I, so badly, wanted to belong somewhere I could feel safe, loved and protected without being judged. I found a small community in Burundi, but I quickly realised that I had to renounce my faith in God and become an extroverted, 'out' person if I was to fit in. I was a young boy, but I already knew that it was not fair to betray the person I was to be accepted by them.

So, in those years of confusion, I started journaling.

Writing provided me with a safe space to cry out loud. I would write how I felt, what I liked, what I hated. I put down on paper all my feelings of sadness, loneliness, frustration, anger and especially my fear of being different. Slowly, I started to write to find myself, to know who I was beyond my family and community's expectations. I was aware that I was nothing like my father, or my cousins, or your 'typical' queer man. I would also read in the hope that I would find in books a male character that I could identify with. Reading other people's stories and writing down my own gave me answers to some of the most complicated questions that I puzzled with. One of the revelations of all this reading and writing was the realisation that I was not weird, or so different – rather, I was a little boy with his own passions, ambitions and a personality that society failed to understand. And that realisation made me happy.

The very loud world we live in makes life really difficult for men and women who do not conform to society's standard gender roles. Girls are expected to be calm and charming; boys strong and brutal; queers either extroverted or hidden away. There's little room for people to find themselves and enjoy whom they discover themselves to be. Too many of us get lost because we do not fit into the boxes that societies and communities have designed for us. Today, I am so lucky I had the courage to step outside. Understanding who I really am gave me my own identity, my own voice, and – most importantly – my freedom.

Divin Ishimwe is a contemporary writer working on non-fiction stories that touch on daily life. He has published a youth book and his essay 'Man in shadow' has appeared in the *Threads and Faces: Stories on Identity and Belonging* anthology published by the African Writers Trust, in partnership with the National Centre for Writing and the British Council, in June 2022.

Sarang – J.D. Stewart

Dylan wanted to meet my parents. I managed to get away with, 'yeah, at some point,' for like, a year. But then he dicked me into submission. You can't ask someone if you can meet their parents while they're inside you. It's not fair. It would have been worse if he'd said 'I love you' while dicking me. The first 'I love you' should be special, right? There should be trumpets. Swans. Waterfalls. Planes flying through the sky, whipping up the clouds into a puffy frenzy. The first 'I love you' shouldn't be normal.

I stare out of the window of the plane as the fields below look like they're going to devour us. I'd say that I miss Scotland but I don't. I enjoy the life we have together. The life we have which is far away from here. He doesn't know what he's getting himself into, but maybe it won't be as bad as I think it will. People only say that when they know it will be worse, don't they?

His head is on my shoulder. He fell asleep as we left Dubai. I don't know how he can sleep on planes and it makes me jealous. The air is thick with sweat and the smell of stale chicken. Dylan ate it. I told him not to. That was the only time he was awake. To eat. His fingers grip mine like he knows we're going down. I like when he sleeps. Watching his eyelids flicker. It's the only time where I feel like I could do anything to him and get away with it. It's the only time he feels like he's mine. He said he couldn't sleep without me next to him. That was two weeks after he left her. I thought things were moving fast but a year has passed and now here we are. Heading home. Well, my home. Not his.

I know my parents won't like him because he's American. He can't help that I suppose. He always said he felt more European. I'm sure they'll love that. Just kidding. They'll hate it. I always mock him when he talks about his white ancestry. Nobody gives a fuck except you, mate. Americans – sorry, no – let me be clearer: white Americans are desperate to be anything other than American. My parents hate shit like that.

Dylan pushes his head deeper into my shoulder. I never thought I'd be someone anyone would want to lean on. I had wanted someone, a moment, a scene like this for as long as I could remember and now I had it. I got the guy. And he's handsome. More handsome than me but we are always our worst critics. Aren't we? We judge and sentence ourselves all the time.

I can see a small amount of drool make its way across his bottom lip and I lean in to kiss it. The man sitting next to him sees me and shakes his head. I look away. My face red. He turns his legs out into the aisle. Trying desperately to get away from us. He's lucky Dylan isn't awake. Dylan would smack his face until there wasn't a face left. I've seen it. I know. He may like guys. Or guy. Me? Only me. But that doesn't mean he won't try and kill you if you act like a homophobe.

Dylan hates labels. I don't know what to call him. He's my boyfriend in my head but then to everyone else I say he's my partner. To my work colleagues he's my friend and to his, I am the same. That's what it's like living in Korea. You have six different versions of yourself you have to present to the world. They don't believe gay is real. They think AIDS doesn't exist in their country. I think that's the thing that fucked me up the most.

When I arrived four years ago, the school I worked for sent me to the hospital for a 'medical check-up'. They do your weight (they said I was fat), height, take a whole bunch of samples just to check your 'vitamins'. That's a lie. They're checking for STDs. More specifically, they're testing for HIV. If you have it, they don't call you, they call the school you work for. The headteacher comes into the classroom and takes you to your apartment, tells you to pack and sends you home. It sounds wild, doesn't it? That's why they think it doesn't exist in Korea. AIDS is not there, they think. One girl got sent home and when she got back to the States she tested again and it was negative. She'd had a false positive. Fucking terrifying. Sitting on a plane the whole way home thinking you have it and you don't. But they own you. They own your visa. Every move you make is under their eyes. So that's why we are different people.

But we are lucky. There are a lot of foreigners (expats) whatever you want to call us who work in the *Hagwon* we are in – a *Hagwon* is a private school. When we asked if we could move in together nobody batted an eyelid. They said if anyone asked, we had to say we were roommates. The neighbours most probably assume different.

The wheels hit the tarmac and my chest goes cold. I want a cigarette even though I gave up. Maybe I'll have to have one. Just one. That's the gateway though, right? He hates when I smoke. He says loads of stereotypical things like: you taste like an ashtray.

Erm.

How would you know? How many ashtrays have you licked recently?

Dylan would get high back in the States all the time. He told me that. When he was in college. That's what he calls university. I think it's cute. Whereas over here, people who go to college are deemed lesser on the social scale of things.

The pilot comes on and tells us we will be taxiing our way to the gate and then we can finally get out of this tin can. I look back at Dylan and he's wide awake. Staring at me.

When did you wake up? I say.

Like, a second ago. Did I drool?

You did. I kissed it away.

Gross.

The man next to him sighs and huffs, ready to blow a house down. Dylan catches it but I pull his face into mine and kiss him. Soft. Brief. Then into his ear: *Ignore him. Please.* He nods, but his eyes are getting angry. That's how it starts.

It looks like a nice day, he says through closed teeth.

It's deceptive. Scotland is like this. It'll be freezing outside. I put some pants on the top of the case if you wanna change.

Don't you mean trousers? Everyone will think you're one of me.

I smile. Kind of. Maybe that's what I want. They'll think I'm not from here. That I don't have the weight of this country inside me. That I carry years of American whiteness instead of Scottish instability and exuberant pride – for something I am not even sure of.

The seatbelt sign turns off and the man next to Dylan moves so fast I think he's a superhero.

What's his problem? Dylan whispers to me. His breath smells of the chicken and an eight-hour flight.

I think he just wants to get out of here, I reply. There's no use in telling him the truth. Saying 'I think he hates gay people' will only make Dylan mad at him and then mad at me for labelling him. Sometimes labels aren't a bad thing. I know they're not. He isn't there yet.

I instantly regret choosing the window and middle seat in Dubai. I hate how people get off of planes. I want to get off fast. I always feel like throughout the journey everyone loses basic common sense and I gain it. Dylan chose the seats – I could have made a point of changing them but he is so excited for this trip, I don't want it to go any way but really well. He did let me choose how we spent the start of it, and so I got to decide that we would stay in a hotel in Edinburgh for a couple of days before going home. I can't deal with finishing the journey from South Korea with heading straight home. With him.

Dylan stands and stretches. His T-shirt rides up and the tuft of hair across his belly and down to his dick glistens with a light smatter of sweat. The woman in the aisle opposite notices, so I put my hand on his stomach and pull the T-shirt down. She doesn't look away, but instead looks at me as if to say: well done. She turns to her husband whose ass crack is on display as he roots around looking for something (I don't know what). She looks back at me and smiles as she pulls his trousers up. As if I would be interested in her man.

Dylan slides himself under the storage locker and pulls out my backpack and then his.

I can carry them, he says.

It's fine. I need mine, it has my passport in it.
Do you think we'll have to wait long at immigration?
No idea. It's early so could be quick. Let's go.

He leads the way and I follow as we exit the plane and get that gust of chilled air I have longed for since the journey began. Scotland has a smell and it hits me instantly. I hope coming back here wasn't a mistake.

Dylan turns and smiles at me, he stretches out his hand and links his fingers into mine. My chest feels cold again as I realise I have never held a man's hand in public here. I try to pull away but he holds me tighter. As we walk through the airport I keep my head down – avoiding the group of lads in some expensive bar drinking pints. It's not that I don't want to be seen holding his hand. I just don't know what it will mean for me to be seen holding his hand if that makes sense.

We get to immigration and he releases me. His body snakes through the stanchions with ease, his passport in his hand. I don't even remember him taking it out of his bag.

There are a couple of people in front of me. I pull out my phone but the battery is dead. It won't work here, that's what I was told. Korea's phone network is on a different frequency completely so you can't even put a different SIM card in. I stare at the picture of me and Dylan. Taken eight months ago on a beach on Jeju Island. We look younger there. His eyes look greener. I feel a hand on my shoulder and turn around. The woman and her ass crack husband are behind me.

You're next, she says. He looks irritated. She probably told him I was gay, right? I don't know.

I go towards the immigration woman, expecting a joyous reception. Four years since I've been home. Welcome

Home, Mr. Tierney. That's what she'll say. Instead, she grunts. I ask her to repeat the question.

Where. Have. You. Come. From. Today.

Wow. People in immigration are so fucking rude, I think as I answer her questions with the disdain she's dishing my way. Finally she stamps my passport and I'm free. Dylan is already on the other side.

I thought you were British? His half smile shows the beginnings of a dimple that never fully made it.

I'm not British. I'm Scottish. And I'm tired. I wasn't paying attention. There's a bathroom round here I think, do you need to go?

He shakes his head and walks over to one of the garish windows, looking at a plane taking off. I've never understood why airports are just windows. They must think people are really horny to see outside.

So this is Scotland? His voice echoes, that booming way Americans do. They have no problem taking up space and making it their own. Even when it isn't.

No. I reply. This is the airport. Scotland is out there. Come on. I need to pee.

He turns around and kisses me.

Thank you for bringing me here. I love you. He turns and walks towards the baggage claim sign and I'm pissed off.

No fountains. No trumpets. No planes in the sky. But right here. In front of a window which basically looks onto a car park. I turn and move quickly to catch up with him.

Dyl, what did you just say?

I love you.

Yeah, I know but we've not said that and you just said it. After a sixteen-hour flight.

I could say it later while I'm fucking you but I know you won't believe it.

Right. It's just not how I expected the first time of you saying that to go.

Sometimes the unexpected is the best way. Don't you think? Come on. Don't be a grumpus. Let's get the fuck out of here. I wanna shower.

We reach the baggage claim and I go to the bathroom. My piss stinks, even though I went to the toilet like a million times on the plane. You know that smell, like it's been inside you for a while and someone finally popped the cap off. The whole bathroom smells that way.

I wash my hands and put water on my face. I look like shit. I defy anyone to fly for as long as we have and not look like shit but there's always someone who manages to beat that, isn't there? Do you hate them as well? I hope so.

When I get out of the bathroom there's quite a large crowd of people. Another plane must have landed. I see Dylan right at the opening of the luggage carousel. He already has my bag.

I'm thankful that it's quiet. Or that everyone is quiet. I haven't been in an English-speaking country for so long I don't know what it would do to my ears. That sounds weird, I know, but when you're surrounded by Korean all the time, it's just nothing but white noise. English is so grating when you're drowning in it all the time. I'm not looking forward to crowds.

Where's your bag? I ask.

No idea. Should be coming soon I guess.

The luggage belt sputters up again, everyone lets out a collective sigh of relief. Nothing worse than losing your luggage. That's why I hate Prague. Because my luggage got lost. Twice.

Bags appear and finally Dylan reaches over and picks his up. He's strong, but I don't remember his bag even being heavy. I reach for mine and he takes it.

You've got the wheels, baby. The dimple appears again. I wish I knew what it was like if it actually reached its potential.

As we reach the exit I begin to slow down. I'm finally home. Not like, home. Obviously. I wasn't born in the airport, but like. This is it. When I step through those doors, I'm back in Scotland and I am still not sure how good I feel about it.

I wish I had told him everything before we left. Maybe I can still do it before we meet my parents. I'm worried in case he stops loving me. It can happen, right? People wake up and just don't love someone anymore. That's why they leave. That's why people end up like torn into a thousand pieces of tiny pink paper and then nobody is there to stick them back together again.

Dylan turns and looks at me.

You OK? He says. He's wanted to come here for like, a year. Sometimes I wonder if that's the only reason he likes me. But there were Scottish girls in Korea, he could have dated one of them, but he chose me. That's what he would say: I chose you. I love you. That's a recent addition, the love. You know that. You witnessed it.

Yeah, I'm good. I think I need something to eat, like. Something proper, I reply.

You need to stop saying 'like' after everything. Your parents will be like, so annoyed. He laughs and I make a sarcastic face at his attempt at a joke.

I could tell him I don't want to step through those doors. I could tell him what happened to me where I grew up.

How I had to leave. How I never wanted to go back there and maybe he'd understand. He told me things. About his mum. How much she drank. It's not the same though. Family drama is baggage we all have. Not everyone went through what I did in school. I don't know what it will be like to walk on those streets I grew up in with everyone seeing him next to me. And he'll hold my hand and I don't want him to. How my parents will look when they meet him. They know I'm gay, but they've never met anyone I dated. Anyone I actually loved. It feels like the final nail in the big gay coffin. I can hear the dirt being thrown on the box. This is it. It's finally happened, they'll think. He's a real life gay now who gets fucked in the ass and sucks cock.

Stephen. Come on, let's go to the hotel. He stretches out his hand and I take it. It will be easier to do this with him by my side, I think. He loves me. He said it in a totally normal way. That's what I hope. That's what I try to tell myself.

J.D. Stewart is a gay writer based in Scotland. He has never written fiction before, as his work has mainly been for the theatre. He hopes that one day you can see this and maybe we can start again.

Elevated People – Lukas Georgiou

The club is full. It's underground. It's dark. It's just one room. We are packed in tight, but not so tight that we can't dance freely and with abandon. And we do dance with abandon. We dance alone, and we dance together. We are gay, we are queer, bi, and lesbian. We are trans, non-binary, and a-gender. We are everything on every spectrum and everything in between. There are even a few straight men here. The room is a rectangle. Small enough to see all four walls, but full enough to be unable to count the hundreds inside.

As I enter, I see a line of dancers raised up above the rest. About twenty of them, a head and body above everyone else, running along a strip in the centre of the room. It's a party, not a show, but eyes are drawn to them, the lights shine on them, their energy is magnetic, and their elevated presence commands our gaze. We all dance, but those elevated people, they dance more. They dance for us, because we are watching. They dance for themselves because they know they can be seen.

*

I work my way through the crowd, mingling here and there. A lot of eye contact, some body contact. Occasionally, I dance with someone, and we engage in something profound: a pairing? an alignment? A courtship. We see each other, we move our bodies separately, in totally different styles, but with the same rhythm, while we look into each other's eyes and smile from ear to ear. Thirty seconds pass, a minute, two. And then we are done. We break eye contact, we cool off, we share a smile, maybe we swap names, and I move on. Their energy enhances me, fills me up, invigorates me, and I want to share it. And so I continue, through the crowd, jiggling, jiving, throwing in moves from different eras and genres. Why not? Who said you can't dance 'Thriller' to Techno? Who said you can't do the Macarena to House? Who said you can't Salsa to Disco?

*

At some point I take my clothes off. But don't worry – I had planned for this moment. I wore something extra special underneath. We all did. As the room heats up, we drip with sweat, and our sweat drips back down on us from where it had condensed on the ceiling. It got so hot that we created steam. So we take our clothes off. It's not that we are simply slutty. It's not just that we are body positive. But our clothes simply must come off. They're just too goddamn wet because we are having just too goddamn much of a good time together.

*

Back from coat-check, in just my Calvin Klein's,
Back from coat-check, in just my tiny pink silk shorts,

182

Back from coat-check, in just my cotton jock strap,
Back from coat-check in just my Speedo,
in just my latex one-piece,
in just my thong,
in just my cock ring,
in just my full-body leather harness,
in just my gimp suit,
in my leotard,
in my ball gown,
in my LBD,
fully naked,
Back from coat-check, in my carefully planned and
    curated outfit,
Back from coat-check, wearing exactly what I was wearing
before because I didn't need to change because I already
looked and felt great, I continue my routine, I continue the
dance, I continue the charade. It's meditation, it's exercise,
it's networking, it's sex, it's love, it's community.

*

Some of us are getting too drunk now. Some of us are get-
ting too high. Some of us are sober and getting tired. We
get high to escape, to liberate our repressed egos, or because
our friends offered stuff for free, or because we are addicted,
or because we are in pain, or just for fun, because we like
the high, to just let loose for joy's sake, because it's easy. We
drink for all the same reasons.

The sober ones are special. They might be incredibly
afraid, or they might be incredibly brave. Both possibilities
are welcomed with joy.

*

I become more curious about the line of elevated people. I had at first assumed that they were a group of performers, dancers, paid to enhance the energy of the room, but now I see that the group has totally changed, it's a different twenty people than it was before. Curious, I make my way through the crowd towards them, jiving, wiggling and bopping between my companions, sliding and rubbing my wet body against everyone else's. I make it to the line. It stretches across the width of the room in front of me, a block of concrete, four feet high, two feet wide, and thirty feet long. The dancers are standing on it. I stare up at them, agog. A bearded man in great gold and black butterfly wings, a woman in platform shoes and a shimmering purple halter neck jumpsuit, someone in clown make-up and a mankini, someone in a body harness made from chains, someone in a grey T-shirt and blue jeans, someone in a patchwork coat of many colours, and it stretches on. I follow the line to one end, the elevated feet near my head, and eventually I reach a staircase leading up to the platform, with a dancer on each step. I shimmy past the three steps, coy. I continue to dance among the crowd, and I watch. The person on the lowest step hops down and embraces me, and the person on the step above them climbs down one. And like this, the line shuffles along, and I realise in that moment what it is. It travels in only one direction. It's a conveyor of sorts. A catwalk. A promenade.

*

I continue my dancing. I am soaked through. I am tired, but I can keep going for a while yet. I feel good. I look good.

My outfit is great. People are saying so. I want it to be seen. And then the inevitable thought crosses my mind.

*

I return from the toilets and make my way to the other end of the conveyor. I do it slowly, remaining interested and directional, yet somewhat aloof and distracted. I make it there, where the dancefloor meets the bottom step. Someone is on it. They look excited, smiling at their friends with confidence, dancing with them, but a step above. Slightly elevated. Slightly Othered. And then the line shuffles along, and the person on the step above them clears, and they step up, and just like that, the first step is empty. I wonder who is going to fill it. I look around, but there's nobody in waiting. Is it my turn already? So soon? I step forward, less coy, asserting myself, but someone else just beats me to it. The grin on their face! I missed my chance . . .

*

But sure enough, a minute passes, and the line shuffles on. The bottom step opens. I wait just two seconds this time, then I step up. *I'm next!* The spirit of the moment enters me and now I am the excited one, the smiling one, the energetic one. And now I'm a foot taller than I was before, and I can see out into the sea of people, and some of them look back at me, and I see my friends and they are smiling at me, willing me on, they know what's coming for me. Were some of them up here before? Are they going to follow?

*

A minute passes, and the step above me clears. I fill the empty space. And now the elevation above everyone else is significant. There's no hiding. The step below me fills up, and now there's no going back. Sure, I could jump off the side, evacuate! But why would I? The line shuffles forward and I step up.

*

And now I'm on the runway. Oh gosh, it's narrower than I thought. Please don't let me fall! Now there really is no going back. It's a performance, a show, a stage, and I'm the latest star.

*

I begin to elevate my performance. The occasion calls for it. Elevated body, elevated mind. I ratchet everything up: my rhythm, my groove, my daring. I really hear the music now. I *feel* it. I feel love. I feel mighty real. Man, I feel like a woman.

*

The line, in its current incomparable incarnation, shuffles along slowly. From up here I can hear the crowd, their voices raised up, chattering, laughing, whooping, moaning, cheering, screaming, chanting, panting. I see and I am seen. I dance for them, whether they see me or not. I dance for myself. It feels good to be brave, to be bold, to put myself out there and up there. My footsteps are precariously close to the edge. I check myself. *Don't get too cocky!* I calm down a little, but I keep dancing, I keep shuffling forward. I see everyone I know, I see those people I courted with earlier, I see a naked person, having the time of their life, I see a person in a wheelchair, having the time of their life, I see two people fucking in the corner, having the time of their lives. I see a couple arguing, their pain drowned out by a thousand joys. I dance for them all. I want to elevate the energy in here. I want to hype everyone up. I take my role seriously! If I'm on this stage, I'll do my damnedest to earn my spot. And it's working! Everyone is dancing now, our energies harmonized. We move as one. People's eyes are drawn to me. Someone points, a friend waves, someone else blows a kiss. And then the person in front of me steps down. I made it to the end. But I was enjoying it so much! Nonetheless, the performance cannot be paused. It's linear and it's participatory. The audience becomes the performers, and the performers become the audience. The energetic exchange is circular. I step down once, twice. I'm on the floor. I hug the closest person to me. I dance a little more, enjoying those whose turn has come on the platform, but soon enough, I exhaust myself. It's 5 a.m.! I better get going. I head out to coat-check.

'Hey!'

Back at coat-check, while I'm re-donning whatever was disrobed, a voice calls. I turn and look up.

'I saw you up there,' he says, 'nice dancing.'

I smile.

Lukas Georgiou is a writer, currently based between London and Berlin. His work centres around hedonism, desire, performativity, excess, and all of the other scintillating aspects of queer life. He is currently writing a speculative fiction novel about gay separatists in a parallel universe.

Phantom Blinks – Ben Skea

dearest PHANTOM BLINKS,

when i chased the sinuous herd syringed into the machine becoming fluorescent the fleshy horizontal scroll of bodies clamped beneath THE IRON PROTECTOR all hot skin and bravado grins rushing in liquid speed my echo eyes scan to you my desire is to become fully augmented amid the loop of moans i guess you too crave aggressive pump and kick deep inside where stuttered neon melts with filthy winks that blur like peppered moths turned black . . .

. . . at 200 bpm outstretched TOMORROWZ LIMBS transmute and grow our new-fangled breathing apparatus grips ribs like an exoskeleton and lips lock-in a suffocating candy-floss kiss synthetic cherry saliva and perforated texture we are SLUTXPLORERS with superior tongue precision i call you SOFTPROBER you tell me your expertise is newfound holes and gaps to fill orbiting inside like a swab forced around the edge of a petri dish picking up remnants mantis-like we pray for rainbow vomit head-rush cool-crush serrated forearms etched in OBSIDIAN OBLIVION . . .

a quick fix shift　　　　　　　　　*for*

　　　　　　　　　　　　　PARALLAX FIENDS.

please find attached :　　　　*(a free pass to fuck)*

love,
HARDCORE RIDER　　　*x*

Ben Skea is an artist who lives and works in Scotland. His practice traverses moving image, experimental animation, sound design and prose poetry. Recent projects have reflected on contemporary anxieties of the body in flux, the fragmented self and the fluidity of realities.

This Day – George Hodson

2021

This day, the devil comes knocking at my door. I'm snug as a bug in a rug in my little home. My two little bronze-coloured Brussels Griffons are curled up on my lap. I'm reading in my armchair when the lights start to flicker. I'm aware there's a storm outside, but having lived in Thailand all those years ago, I don't take storms in London seriously. Then from nowhere, water begins to seep up through the floor, through the carpet. And it isn't water. It's raw sewage.

It's seeping into every room in my basement flat. It quickly reaches one metre in depth. The stench is unbearable. My little dogs are swimming in it. They're swimming for their lives, screeching, and because of my poor hands, I can't catch them. And I'm hit by a sense of terror and trauma that I've never had before in even the darkest days of my illnesses. I'm seventy-two and I'm watching the destruction of my world. My pictures, my diaries, my keepsakes, my memories, my dogs – we're all drowning. The safe haven where I've battled so many trials of life is being washed away in shit. Everything starts to crash down.

1984

This day is a festival in Thailand called Loy Krathong, celebrating the mother river goddess. People make little boats from banana leaves, and place a candle and a coin on them, then say a prayer as they set them off to float downriver. This day is beautiful, and it's one of my first dates with Sam. The two of us embark on a small boat and it's just exquisite. It's night-time, and there are just thousands of these little boats with candles floating on the water. I can't imagine anything more romantic. The stars hang above all these little prayers. I'm excited because festivals have always fascinated me, and to be sharing this one with my new love is even more exciting. I'm really geared up for this date.

Sam shows me the little banana-leaf boat he's made, and when it's time to light the candle and set it off on its journey, Sam kisses me. He says, 'My prayer is that we're together forever.' He places it down on the water and off it floats. We cuddle and watch his prayer float away and mingle with thousands of others.

1991

This day, I'm troubled. I'm trying to get my love Sam to come to London and look after me. Now that I'm living with AIDS and cancer, he's desperate to come and join me from Thailand. We've already been apart for four months.

I've been living with friends, sleeping on their couches, but I've developed a non-Hodgkin's lymphoma and I need more support. Despite the fact that Sam has an MA from an American university, speaks fluent English and is a trained teacher of deaf children, the Home Office has rejected his application. The lawyer explains to me that because he's from Thailand, officials fear he is coming with the intention of being a prostitute.

I don't want to carry on living if I can't have Sam beside me. It pushes me to one of my darkest places, knowing that institutions like the Home Office can be so cruel. I write to Chris Smith, the only openly gay MP, and beg for his help. He takes up the case and we challenge the Home Office's position. They say he isn't allowed to work, or receive benefits, but he can come for six months due to the exceptional circumstances. *See you soon, Sam.*

1993

This day, Sam and I are going down to Peter and Angela's, my parents. I really don't want to go. But Sam, being much more family-orientated than I am, says we should visit them. I haven't seen them for ages, and not since telling them that I have a diagnosis of AIDS.

We're walking down the lane to the house, and I feel dread about seeing these wretched people. When we arrive they're already half-cut on gin. There's a look of fear in their eyes. They don't touch me, they don't hug me. Peter is too drunk to realise how loud he is when he says to Angela, 'Oh god, he's not only queer. He's also married a wog.'

I'm ready to leave, but Sam calms me, and we stay.

Angela serves a pork loin, with a creamy mushroom sauce, red cabbage and beautiful creamed potato. Over dinner Peter starts talking about Thailand. He says to Sam, 'It's full of prostitutes, isn't it?'

Just as I'm eating my pudding, I notice on the back of my spoon a dot of red nail polish. I look at all my other utensils and plates. There's a red dot on every item that Sam and I are using.

1994

This day, Sam and I are being offered to take AZT, a failed chemotherapy drug that may help to control our HIV. I intuitively feel that I won't, I can't. Sam decides to take it. The doctors have no idea about AZT's toxicity and the cumulative effect of taking it. So, Sam and all the other people living with HIV who are on AZT receive massive doses. And over a period of six months or so, I notice Sam begin to fade. First his energy levels fall. He loses weight. I can't understand it, because this isn't happening to me, even though we both have HIV. Deep down inside, I think: is the HIV starting to take Sam, or is it a side effect of the drug?

This day, Sam is meticulously cutting his beautiful black hair in the bathroom mirror. It's a ritual of his: he has a wonderful crewcut, which he keeps very neat, and a dark moustache. When I enter the room, he turns to me and says, 'It's starting to show, darling, isn't it?'

I take him in my arms. Because I love him, I can't lie. I say, in his ear, 'Yes. I'm afraid it is starting to show.' We both cry a deep, deep cry. You don't lie to people you love.

As I hug him I can feel his bones. An inner, primal scream of anger boils up inside me that this vile, vicious virus and this unknown drug are taking Sam away from me.

Within three months you had died. Oh, Sam.

2012

This day, I'm cleaning out my closet. I'm a bit of a hoarder, so in I must go. When I get to the very bottom of the closet I find something magic. My lovely partner Sam has been dead for eighteen years, but the grief never goes away. And there at the very bottom in the corner is a little brown box – it's Sam's watercolour box, and it's been there for eighteen years. I open the box and inside is a plastic tray of palettes.

These little trays are made to hold different colours, but in Sam's, inside each palette is an exquisite little painting. I run my fingers over them, thinking of how Sam had made some little paintings here. And I realise these are the same colours he used on the Valentine's card he made for me just a month before he died. It's with this simple watercolour box that I remember Sam, and I say to myself, 'You're not gone, you're still here, you're still near me.'

2022

This day, I'm in a pickle. For forty years my only work has been survival – HIV, four consecutive cancers, heartbreak and a heart bypass, the recent awful pandemic, and then the flood of sewage last year that nearly wiped me and the dogs out. Now I'm in my council flat at seventy-three, and I'm getting a bit wibbly wobbly. No money, no pension. I don't have a pot to piss in, and it's disturbing me. I'm thinking about who I'd call if I fell down or if the flood of sewage rises again. If I'm incapacitated, I'll be shuffled off to some stinky bog-standard state nursing home. Many of the people there won't understand what an out-and-loud, queer warrior queen with HIV is. I won't be able to be who I really am. They'll make me sit and listen to Vera Lynn on a loop.

So this day I've got to find a way around this. I'm sitting at home having a dream. And the dream is a community centre for people living with HIV and a cluster of retirement homes for elder warrior queens like me who don't have any money. Our community is strong and loving. We are powerful activists and organisers, and we have allies who want to help. This day I'm feeling that creating this living AIDS memorial is my next big challenge. Now that I'm cancer-free, with blessings, and still high-kicking, I'll put my energy and love into trying to make this dream come true.

George Hodson is an interdisciplinary artist, HIV activist, and breeder of award-winning Griffon Bruxellois. His memoir will be published later this year by Polari Press. ghodsonart.wordpress.com

Self-Portrait as Sappho in Love –
Nikki Ummel

It's the hard nipples for me.
No. The soft hairs that surround   hard nipples,
my thumb   rotating counter-clockwise
as my fingers cup the rest of her breast. Again and
   again and
     sometimes I cup my own but   it's never the same.

The thrill of you under me quite so new.   The Squirm.
No. The lead up to The Squirm.   Social media
   stalking and flirty texts.
  Bar drinks that lead to waist-touches, your big love-
   crumb eyes
    and one of us slow-pushing the other against
   the wall   below the darts.
 A beer spilled.   The probable *get a room.*   Yes.

In the room,
   muscles better and nerves buzz.   The soft-firm-electric
of new lips. On my hand.   My tongue.   My

inner thighs.
How you know my scars.
How you lick them. Again and again and again.

Where the Earth Runs Red –
Nikki Ummel

Promise me
　　　　you'll pluck　　my tongue & teeth
　to wear on a string
　　that slides between your breasts
　　　while you smash the china I left
　　　　　　　　　　　　　at your house, accidentally.
　　　Finger the sandpaper edge of my tongue
　　while you arc back as
she　　makes you come.

　　　Kiss me with her clit on your lips
　　　　so I can taste　　what I am missing.

　　　　　　Your eyes, black,
　　　　　　　slice the grainy pane of her back
　　　　　window. With my thumb I trace
　　　　　　the imprint of your　　palm sweat sweet
　　but you turn away,
　　draw the shades.

Tell me again
how we used to laugh,
   throat-deep after midnight,
      too drunk to sleep,
         too awake to think

                      this would last.
          Tell me what it felt like
       when we slept in the desert
    during that freak rainstorm,
      how we corner-stacked our bags &
     played king of the hill
  as the lightning struck
the sky a punctured bruise.

Nikki Ummel is a queer writer, editor, and educator in New Orleans. Nikki has been published or has work forthcoming in *Painted Bride Quarterly*, *The Adroit Journal*, *The Georgia Review*, and others. She has been nominated for a Pushcart Prize, Best New Poets, Best of the Net, and twice awarded the Academy of American Poets' Andrea Saunders Gereighty Poetry Award. She is the 2022 winner of the Leslie McGrath Poetry Prize. She has two chapbooks, *Hush* (Belle Point Press, 2022) and *Bayou Sonata* (NOLA DNA, 2022). You can find her on the web at www.nikki-ummel.com.

Studio – Amy Ridler

The buzzer interrupts the grey curve of the line, ending it prematurely. Kay puts down their pencil and surveys the room. This isn't the first time that hours have been lost to drawing. The plan was to tidy up a bit before she arrived. On the way to the receiver, Kay collects discarded plates and a few too many half-drunk, then forgotten about, coffee cups. It's too late to wash them now; they go into the cupboard under the sink, neatly stacked. To be dealt with later. The buzzer sounds again. Kay picks up the receiver, presses the button but does not speak. The little green light, which indicates the door is open, blinks. Kay turns and scans the studio. They push the stack of old magazines, saved for collaging, under the desk with their foot and straighten the rug so it is in line with the coffee table. Windows open, Kay couldn't remember their last shower. Two, maybe three days ago. Despite the sun blazing through the blinds, Kay lights a few scented candles to freshen things up.

The groan of the lift doors opening send a jolt of nervousness through Kay's body. Walking to the door, Kay strains to hear any noise from outside but it is silent. Eyes closed, Kay breathes out and counts to ten. When there is still no knock, they start to wonder whether it was her at all. She didn't give a specific time, *sometime in the afternoon*. People were often in and out of the studio block, it could have been a mistake – maybe one of the other artists had forgotten their key. Kay tiptoes closer to the studio door, now inexplicably feeling like an intruder in familiar surroundings. Looking through the peephole Kay can clearly see Hazel in the communal landing. She is looking at herself in the reflection of the giant windows that overlook the canal. Hazel smooths her hair down. She flicks it all over to one side, but instantly pulls it back down over both shoulders and ruffles the front. She tucks her T-shirt into her jeans and looks at herself from the front and then the side. Kay could open the door, but it feels like a moment that shouldn't be disturbed. Besides, Kay has been looking for far too long now and doesn't know if they can open the door and convincingly pretend to be surprised to see Hazel standing there. Hazel takes a little bottle out of her bag that Kay can't quite make out. Perfume. She sprays it behind her ears and walks towards the door. Kay jumps back, holding their breath as the knock finally arrives.

In the time it takes Kay to compose themselves and open the door, Hazel has untucked her T-shirt again: it falls loosely at her waist.

– Hello.

– Hey, sorry I didn't text to say I was on my way. I figured you would be in all day so –

– Yeah, it's cool. It'll be nice to have a break. Come on in.

Hazel steps over the threshold and into the space ahead of Kay. Coconut fills the air as she passes but, within seconds, settles on a muted woody aroma that Kay recognises as 'her smell'. Seeing the place through someone else's eyes makes Kay self-conscious.

– Sorry, it's a little cramped in here. I forget. It's usually just me.

– Don't entertain in here much?

Hazel's mocking tone puts Kay at ease. Her face is warm.

– Oh yeah, all the time. Wild parties every night.

The two of them stand facing each other. Kay realises that there is no obvious place for Hazel to sit. Over in the corner by the window, Kay notices that the bed is still unmade from this morning. It's a single bed, not used very much. Not until recently. *Artists are not permitted to make the studios their permanent residence.* Kay remembers the reminder that came through the door last month. *Artists are permitted to work on their craft through the night, but they must not treat the studios as a home.* No one would find out. The bed doubles up as a sofa. A tie-dye throw is draped across the mattress and there are cushions along the back wall – when they came for the inspection, the landlord didn't notice anything out of the ordinary, or chose not to.

Hazel walks over to the desk to look at the cuttings tacked up above. Ideas, inspiration for projects, test sheets. The walls are covered. Kay seizes this moment to make the bed presentable, swiping the empty biscuit wrapper from the floor on their way past.

– Would you like a drink? Tea, coffee? Whisky?

– Oh, what are you having?

– I was going to have a tea.

– Thank god. Yes, I'll have the same. I was hoping you weren't going to have a whisky because then I'd feel boring if I didn't have one too.

– You don't want one?

– It's a bit early.

Kay raises an eyebrow in mock shock before picking the kettle up and heading to the door.

– There's no water in here. It's just down the hall in the communal kitchen. Won't be a sec.

Kettle filled; Kay is just about the push the studio door open when they feel a wave of nervousness. That same feeling when Hazel arrived. Leaving Hazel in the studio alone felt strange, exposing. Hazel's back is to Kay when they re-enter. She is crouched down behind the plants looking at some miniature sculptures that Kay never got round to finishing.

– These are beautiful.

– Take one if you like. I started something with them, but they've been sitting there for a year. Have one.

– What? I couldn't!

– If you like them, take one with you. No one else has ever set eyes on them. I forgot I'd even made them.

Kay takes two clean mugs from the cupboard. When they look back at Hazel, she has returned to the bed with one of the ceramic figures in her hand. She is smiling down at it as if holding a rare jewel. This makes Kay smile too, but they are careful to turn back to the worktop before Hazel looks up.

*

The mugs, long drained of tea, now contain whisky. There was nothing satisfactory to mix it with. Kay cut up a lime and placed a wedge in each mug. The sun is gone, but the air is still warm. A few more candles are lit as the sky turns from orange to indigo. The only lamp Kay owns is on the desk, too far away to be of any use. As they leave the day behind, Kay notices Hazel relax. She'd taken her boots off, hours ago now, and has her feet tucked under herself, head resting on the wall. She is talking too, much more freely than when she arrived.

– I don't know what's more depressing. Watching people drink their money away, become more and more annoying, you know? I know that makes me sound judgemental, but it's not that. When I'm pouring their fifth round of tequilas all I want to do is jump over the bar and join them. What's worse? That, or standing in the shop all day having people buy a single piece of lingerie that costs more than my whole day's wages?

Kay takes a sip of their whisky. This is a new, more open version of Hazel. She is less guarded, and Kay finds that the more she says, the more Kay wants to know. She is sick of working part-time jobs to make ends meet. Frustrated at her situation. That makes two of them. She tops up her mug and continues.

– I hope that things pick up soon. I get a few good gigs here and there, but not enough to support myself. Not yet anyway.

Kay can sympathise, though they don't say too much. *In your forties and what do you have to show for it?* These thoughts aren't helpful, Kay knows where thoughts like this lead, and they aren't in a hurry to go back there. Hazel lists all of the reasons why her jobs are crushing her soul. She rarely makes eye contact, which allows Kay to really take her in. Her dark brown hair curls around her face, framing it in the candlelight. Kay has never seen it like this. Earlier in the evening, she had apologised for her 'wild hair'. Kay said she looked gorgeous either way. A pained squeak was all that they had got in return. Unsure how to take this, Kay had changed the subject.

For most of the evening, Hazel sat with her arms curled around her knees, pulling them into her chest, protective. Every so often, she would forget herself. Her arms would wave around in the air, releasing her knees from the vice like grip. Suddenly, mid-sentence, she would realise she was doing this and go back to her default position. The frequency of this increased as the whisky disappeared. Seeing that switch flicker on and off amused Kay.

– What?

Hazel's question snaps Kay back to reality. They don't know the answer, but Hazel is staring straight at them, waiting for a response.

– You're smirking! Why!?

Kay relaxes, detecting that same mocking tone from earlier. Caught in the act. They had long stopped listening to Hazel. It was hard to concentrate on her words, when their own head was swimming with questions. *Where could this go? What could it be?*

Last week, at the end of their third date, Kay had plucked up the courage to tell Hazel they had just started taking testosterone. They had been putting it off, unsure how Hazel would react; after all, she was interested in women. It had built up and up in Kay's head, expecting Hazel to end things the moment she knew. True to form, Hazel's expression was unreadable. She asked no questions and nodded along as Kay rambled through a list of reasons why it was essential.

– You don't have to justify it to me. It's your body.

The following day, Hazel had dropped by, unan- nounced, to the cafe Kay had been picking up a few shifts at. Kay hadn't noticed her until she was right up at the counter and by that time, it was too late to fix their hair or take off the apron they were wearing. Hazel said she couldn't stop, but she wanted to drop off a little gift.

– Don't open it 'til I'm gone.

Kay could think of little else for the rest of the shift. With no one to cover the floor, the package, wrapped in brown paper, sat on the shelf above the till. Two hours passed and with each minute Kay became more impatient. Finally, after what felt like days, Kay was released. The temptation to run straight to the bathroom, to rip it open then and there, was strong but they resisted. Savouring the moment just that bit longer, they cycled home at top speed.

A shaving kit. A vintage shaving kit. 1940s Kay thought. Beautiful. The original razors were still tucked in, wrapped in tissue paper with print too faded to read. This was the real deal, enclosed in a tan leather case. Kay had just started taking T, there wasn't a hair on their face, but the gesture was beyond anything they could have imagined. Hazel really saw Kay, saw what they wanted. She was unsure of herself, but she was trying to learn and learn quickly.

Kay wiped away tears with the back of their hand as they took each piece out, one by one to look at in the pink glow of the setting sun.

The memory swam around in their head, but the line taking up most of the space: *She won't stay. It won't last.*

– I'd better get going anyway. Now that I've bored you into submission with all the reasons I can't go back to work, I better go to bed so I can—

She smiles and puts her hand on Kay's knee, squeezing slightly as she steadies herself up.

– So, I can get up for work.

She groans again. Kay is growing quite fond of that little groan. Still unsure of each other, Kay stands, hovering, as Hazel ties up her boots, gathers her things. Kate Bush continues to sing from the record player in the corner of the room, filling the silence. Hazel doesn't look up; she checks her bag and her pockets and walks over to the door.

– It's late. Are you heading home soon? We could walk together.

– I've got a couple of things to finish here.

Kay knows that they need to say more.

– I've got an early meeting here, so I might just crash on the sofa. Had a few too many whiskys to be cycling home tonight.

This seems to satisfy Hazel. She stands in the doorway but says nothing. Kay looks at her and wonders why the hell she wants to spend her time here.

– It was really great to see you. Thanks for stopping by. Next time I'll take you somewhere better than a grubby studio.

– I love it here.

Kay can taste the lime on Hazel's lips as she breaks away. She stays close. They look at each other, and Kay realises how little eye contact Hazel ordinarily makes. Her eyes flicker around the room, settling on her hands, or the floor but rarely at Kay. A smile spreads across her face as her gaze retreats over Kay's shoulder.

– I better go.

She stands by the lift and Kay can't bring themself to shut the door, not just yet. They watch as Hazel presses the button impatiently even though they can both hear the lift on its way up. When the doors of the lift open, Kay waves.

Hazel runs back over, kisses Kay on the nose and is gone before Kay can react.

*

Candles have been blown out and only the violet light from the sky aids Kay now. As they climb into the small bed, their feet touch on the cold stone wall. No curtains: the sun will be up soon. Kay looks around. *What does she love about this?* Scraps of paper tacked to every wall; records piled up in crates in the corner. Each piece of furniture has either been found or made. Nothing matches. The shelves at the foot of the bed look like they could collapse at any given moment. Kay's eyes are drawn towards the bottom shelf, where the ceramic miniatures sit. Kay pulls the blanket up around their neck and smiles again as they notice the space where one is missing.

Amy Ridler is a writer and English Teacher in East London, where she runs the LGBT+ society. She is currently the Managing Editor of MIR Online. She has worked with queer, feminist, live art theatre company Carnesky Productions as an Associate Artist since 2009 and continues to be a member of the advisory board.

Shopping for a Can of Moondance – Betty Benson

after Jeanne Wagner

I cannot explain to the clerk in Lathrop Paint:

what the body remembers at night,
in bed, watching through windowpanes,
as the moon rises over the trees,
spills its smooth honey milk over white
linen sheets and onto the floor. This is the light
I want to brush my walls – lily of the valley, warm
fog, champagne –
borrowed light I cannot hold.

In my hand the perfect paint chip: Moondance
(unavailable, discontinued).

*

What I know by heart I could not have imagined
that night we rose from our beds
after a warm rain and walked
into mid-summer moonlight. You
took my hand – we
danced, two barefoot
silhouettes splashing into our broken-
glass reflections: the stars dangled, tiny
silver charms falling all
around, our breath, white
whispers in rain-
washed air.

I cannot explain
the ways our bodies moved
as our edges dissolved
in white-washed mist,
how we danced until cloud shadows
covered the moon.

*

To the blank-eyed clerk holding shards of colour:

I only want what you can never
give me; the unavailable, the discontinued,
the break–your–heart–forever

Moondance. Put away
your white dove and pearl, your frostline
and cotton; don't show me the parchment,
the alabaster, or the bone.

Betty Benson (she/her) is an educational psychologist who lives and writes in the United States. Her work has appeared in or is forthcoming in *Of Rust and Glass* (LGBTQIA Fiction Anthology), *RockPaperPoem* and *As Above So Below*.

Find Your Animal –
Swithun Cooper

Listen: that's him, on the staircase down into the scullery. His hesitant tread like someone might rush up and push him aside at any moment. So, turn – turn quickly from the stove, leave the lentils steeping – and meet him as he steps in through the doorway. Feel the cool of his body inches from yours. Move back so he can come fully into the room. Now tap your finger on the photograph taped to the wall, beside the calendar.

Say: Look. Look how good we look.

Don't tell him – not yet – that you've never been able to stand yourself in pictures before. How much you've hated your face, its wonky smile, or the way people always said you stood like a sissy. As a child, on holidays, at Christmas, you'd hide when the camera came out, and once, caught off guard, you ducked behind the dog. For years your mother brought that one out laughing to show people.

Instead, keep your finger on this photograph, cut from the report on the protest in today's *Argus*. Point to the picture's centre: you. Touch where your top has ridden up, where, under its hem, your soft belly hangs exposed. Touch the torn neckline revealing the mousy hairs on your chest, a few of them already grey. The tendons on your neck in this picture are straining like they might split the skin from beneath.

Prod his image. His walking boots and leopard print dress. Laugh at the ragged state of the two of you. Prod the cop who has you arm locked. Prod the cop who has him arm locked. Slide your fingertip over to where, as you both strain away from the cops, his mouth meets yours. Your chin, where his blood is smeared.

Say: People keep asking, did I cut my lip?

When he smiles – and he will smile, he's smiling a lot today, proud to show his newly broken tooth – smile back. Wonky as ever. Don't try to change it.

*

But as you do this, remember he doesn't know what this photograph means to you. He doesn't know that until now you've always chosen to be in the background. You're one of the squat's originals – you and Jen and Ryan did the research last summer, found the old nunnery, empty for years, that had passed between developers and been somehow forgotten – but you're not one of its figureheads. Jen made the zines and posters, you photocopied them. Jen spoke at rallies, her language rich with love for this radical queer collective she was forming, inviting people to squat at the nunnery with her, and you checked her mic beforehand, then dashed off-stage. While Ryan was choosing outfits to host the cabarets and riot grrrl shows, styling her flat-top and box fade so nobody knew if she was a butch or a boy, you were getting the generators working, rubbing mint leaves on the skirtings to keep away mice, stinging your forearms as you ripped out the nettles that had grown through the nunnery's brickwork. They stride, visible. You walk with your shoulders hunched. For years you've worn this same black cotton jacket, secure in how it makes eyes pass across you.

He doesn't know all that. Doesn't know that the first night he came here, to one of Ryan's punk gigs, you saw him right away. Standing alone with his thin yellow hair unstyled and unwashed. He kept wiping his moustache with the back of his wrist – you could tell it was new and still itching him. The desire to belong shone out of him, and so did the fear that he wouldn't. Helping out all that night, you kept thinking: I can go over, I'm one of the originals, I'll hand him a Red Stripe as a welcome, it won't have to feel humiliating if he doesn't like me back –

And then of course by the time you'd worked up the courage, he was gone.

You could tell him now. What you know. What Jen said.

But there's already so much you haven't told him. You've never said how glad you were when he came back. More gigs. More meetings. He started sleeping in the old chambers. You, meanwhile, carried on with the vegetable garden, sat in discussion groups about internalised hierarchy, tried to work with nature rather than harness it to your needs. You hauled gear and ran the soundchecks for cabarets, and afterwards, when everyone partnered off in twos and threes, you lay on the mildewed sofa in the old prayer room and read *The One-Straw Revolution*.

You spoke to him of course. But it's scary, to want. To want, for the first time, to be seen. So you said nothing.

*

Now, here in the scullery, as his eyes linger on the picture, say it. Say: I'm glad we found our animals in time.

And when he replies – when he says, what? *Now we have to keep them*, perhaps – remember this was not only his first protest. This was his protest.

He was the one who brought it in: a printout from some local online news site. He read it aloud to the group. Part report, part interview. Down by the viaduct three men had approached two boys: students, both nineteen, leaving a gay bar at 2 a.m. high on MDMA. The men asked something about drugs, the boys paused, it began. One boy got a kick to the head that fractured his temple. The other broke a rib that, on X-Ray, had nearly pierced a vital organ. These boys told the website that the men had said *fucking faggots* over and over as they kicked.

He waved the printout. It's right there, he said, see? *Fucking faggots*. They've written it, they've starred out fucking, but not faggots.

Nobody – not you, not Jen – had heard him speak for this long. Usually he was quiet: sat as a disciple while Jen spoke, closely watching the movement of her hands, writing down the terms she used on his palm in biro.

It was deep, his voice, and soft even though he was furious.

So these men are spinning it as a drug deal gone wrong, he said. And there's even a quote from some right-wing councillor: 'these are spurious accusations by people whose memories of the event have, by their own admission, been affected by Class A drugs. These young men got into a fight and now they're using identity politics as a weapon.'

They'll get off, he said. Do we fight? Help these two boys appeal?

Jen snatched the printout from him, rolled her eyes. What, and protest for a re-trial? The prison system being so famous for all its good work at tackling homophobia. That's liberation to you, is it, locking others up?

You watched him shrink, hating his mistake, desperate to get back on her good side.

You thought it then, but you didn't tell him: Jen's fearlessness charms people, but it also hurts. She's cruel to those who fail to keep pace with her freedoms. She loves her body – including the mole sprouting hair on her jaw, the crooked grey tooth at the front of her mouth – and considers your own lack of confidence a moral failing. A capitalist hangover, she says: appearances are the currency of a rotten marketplace.

No. Don't say it. She matters so much to him.

Instead, perhaps, tell him that seeing his embarrassment was why you stepped in. Why you asked him, did he want to organise a protest? And did he need to find his animal?

*

Or, maybe, ask him about Ryan's clothes. Had he really not seen the room upstairs? Hadn't he wondered, when she left with just one bag – split from Jen and moved to Glasgow – where all those wigs and heels from her cabarets went, the sweat-smelling dresses, the make-up cases smeared with powdery fingerprints?

Animal drag, she called it. Drag for when a gang gets together, gets drunk and fearless, coats their mouths with red gashes, wipes face paint thick across their eyelids. Covers everything in glitter.

Admit it to him now: when you led him to that room, it was your first time too.

219

Here, you said to him. Time to find an outfit that makes you feel dangerous. Vile. A nightmare vision of who they think we are.

Then what? he asked.

Then on the day of the hearing, when they're released, we go down and rush them. Us acting like that – it's like leeches, it brings the fever to the surface. If they're homophobes, that's when they'll expose themselves. They'll show everyone who they really are, whatever the court says.

But will that even change anything?

It teaches them they might have won the court case, but if they think they're free to do it again, we know. And we have our own power.

Maybe, he said, maybe Jen's right. We should be building something away from all that. Invite those two poor boys into our world.

Almost in a whisper, you said: Sure. But what you want for them is revenge. Right?

A shiver ran through your groin as you said it, and again, as he looked up and smiled candidly. After all, by then Jen had already come round to the idea, was getting the word out, getting people angry. As the week went on the group spent hours making banners, someone sourced a sound system bike and everyone chose songs for it. And you and he drank homemade wine, got boisterous, went through Ryan's bags of drag.

Is that all you want to tell him, really? That although you hid it, when he pulled off his jumper to put on a dress, dropped his black trousers uncaring, it made you think you could do the same. When you pulled dresses out and described them to him, acted knowledgeable and unaffected, actually, you'd never done it before. You just knew

Ryan did that and you were imitating her. She gave all her outfits names. Patti. Nina. Deb. See what the outfit's telling you, she said, and what it turns you into, then name it. That's your animal.

You could ask him now: does he remember? How he pulled on that neon leopard print dress and said instantly, Oh, she's a wild time. Determined to be herself. Won't be demure just because it's expected of her.

You matched it, then, with thick-soled walking boots. Good for stamping. He put you in a thin blouse with a pussy bow neckline, which he tied for you, laughing. It was tight at the back and it clung to the fat on your flank. Your belly hung over the waistline of the black sequin shorts you'd put on.

Does he remember saying, What are you calling her?

And you replying: My animal? This one's Lilith. Lilith Thatcher. Pristine with a capacity for evil.

The leopard print dress gaped to his sternum and the bones of his chest heaved. He tore out the sponge pads sewn into the breast. The fabric hung loose, swung when he walked, exposed one nipple and then the other. Laughing he coloured them in with glittery lipstick.

How much you wanted to put your finger there. To wipe some of it off him and smear it on your lips.

*

Is it now? Is now the time to speak?

To ask if he remembers how warm your hands were, gripping each other, both of you shaking with nerves as those men left the courthouse? How he held on to you as the troupe came from all angles, blowing whistles, screaming, and everyone wearing monster drag?

Ask him, was it during that chaos – when you descended, heard those men crying *What the fuck* – and when eight of you linked arms and closed round them, high-kicking, chanting, shrieking – when, as you knew they would, they spat *fucking fags, you faggots, get the fuck off me* –

Was it when one of those men punched him hard in the mouth, knocked him face-first on the pavement – and you swung a kick at that fucker so your heel skinned the back of his hand, made sure he was bleeding too –

Was it then that he found her? Was that what made him able to see that man's red knuckles and grab them, cradle them briefly, kiss them softly?

Or was it during the armlock that came next – how he strained away from the cop to kiss you in front of everyone, as a sign of protest – and you felt completely beautiful –

Was it then that he found his animal, knew her name?

*

Afterwards the cops let you free with a warning. He'd looked down, swept dirt off the lap of his dress. Fearless, he'd said, wants to be herself whatever. It's Jen, isn't it. My animal. She's Jen. Jennifer.

So tell him now – here in the steam of the scullery – tell him how Jen laughed when you informed her of this. Tell him she said, Oh god, I never should have fucked him that first night. I was only hurt because me and Ryan were splitting up. And now he's my shadow and I'm his animal.

*

No. Don't say it.

He is inches away. You both stand on the threshold of each other.

All you need to do is point to the photograph taped to the wall and tell him. Not in so many words. Just let him see. He has made you able to look at yourself. He made you enjoy being looked at, however briefly.

Step away. Smile.

Say: Look how good we look.

Say: Look.

Swithun Cooper has published stories about squats, sex, and anarchism in *A Queer Anthology of Healing* (Pilot Press) and *Unreal Sex* (Cipher Press), and poems in magazines including *Magma*, *Poetry London* and *The North*. He has won an Eric Gregory Award and in 2020 he was an emerging writer in residence at the London Library.

Vanilla – Tom Bland

I burnt the books I was given at Christmas   the
      novels that sold a million   copies   each
detailing the lives of boring heterosexual people
their stories were already inside me
                              why you may ask
    an exorcism of what we are   force fed from birth to
                death

I have always wanted to die on some   level
to leave a hole in
the ground   so eyes could   peer in and see *my* stories
      the ones I never told   in the curvatures of
    where my body was   meant to be

My tears always taste of my favourite   ice cream
                            vanilla

I am a hole in the mirror   which my hand wrapped
    around a
screwdriver made when
      I was off my tits on what was
meant to be e but was a speed ball crystallised in a red
pill that made my mind explode into shards of quartz

A Patchwork of Private Madness was a book I read but I
    couldn't
remember
anything except the title so I tried to write what I imagined
the words were

      Cock tastes good   is it weird to taste your own
cum in another's mouth   our semen mix together

     it's alchemical
it's what Paracelsus was after
                  the act of coalescing
     poisons as elixir

No one reads Paracelsus anymore but then again
      no one tries to exorcise
                the non–consensual stories
     branded into
        their brains

I just want to kiss and fuck and drink champagne and take
every conceivable
     mind-bending drug but at
the same time never stop   processing
    never stop realising   the hole of
    research has no end   we just fall

FUCK ME I THINK A LOT

      I should be doing something for money
I should be analysing dreams or thinking of card designs or
         writing novels

to make   to burst   open   something new in

    a world caught in nostalgia
hanging on the edge of the apocalypse like cows trapped
in a field seeing the lightning coming

     That cow image comes from the fact I found a
steak half price
    in Iceland today   I fried it just enough
to feel the squishy
     meat against   my tongue

I remember going to Gay's The Word at 17 and as I walked
out two lads started whispering
faggot in my ear   they were so close to me   I could
smell the Lynx
    after seeing the sex art books
         I just wanted them to take me down

        an alleyway and fuck me

I don't want to save humanity   we are doomed to be tiny
semiconscious beings that have an
overwhelming desire to   fuck and think   to quote
the words   of Paracelsus

ALL IS QUEER
IN THE COSMOS

which he had a man   in a leather hood   cut
into   his buttocks   with a red–hot blade
    to turn   the
    voices   into love

Tom Bland's *Camp Fear* and *The Death of the Clown* are published by Bad Betty Press. He has a strange life and is currently writing his next book.

Sagittal – Jonathan Kemp

I write this very decidedly out of despair over my body and over a future with this body.

I was in a difficult situation; an urgent journey lay before me. I couldn't travel, of course, I was far too ill. Even without the Great Containment I was clearly going nowhere. I lay there shivering and sweating, sweating and shivering, for what felt like centuries. I was being educated in the experience of deep time, no longer a citizen of this stricken planet, but of some hazy interzone lacking any known coordinates.

The urgent journey I wouldn't be making was to Prague, to deliver a paper at an academic conference on the themes of Sickness and Enlightenment. I'd prepared to talk about Kafka's story, 'A Country Doctor', in relation to the emergence of the clinical gaze and the Homosexual Death Drive.

Every illness is an opportunity to reconfigure the social map. As Freud tells us, the way in which we gain new knowledge of our organs during painful illnesses is perhaps a model of the way by which in general we arrive at the idea of our body.

Consciousness is an illness.

Take off his clothes, they said, then he will heal, and if he doesn't, kill him.

Imagine, this wounded male is going to watch his family undress the doctor and carry him over to the bed and lie him down next to him. Before long, that injured boy is going to coax the handsome doctor into acts of a sexual nature the man of medicine has never done before, though the boy is clearly very well-versed in these dark arts, it would seem, the way he leans in and whispers in the older man's ear, pressing his lips close to the skin, you can tell he's done this before; and the way not a single member of the boy's family, who are present in the room watching the doctor undress and climb into bed with their ailing, wounded son, not one of them bats an eyelid. You just know they've seen it all before, perhaps even enjoy watching it, though each face remains blank and impassive – or so I imagine.

At the fever's peak – around the twenty-seventh day, I believe, though my thoughts were so frenzied I could be wrong, and I made no notes – I had to change my pyjamas and bedding half a dozen times in a single night, and then night after night for nearly a week. So deserted by myself, by everything. Noise in the next room. Locks all over my body.

As bacteria battled with my heavily compromised immune system, fucking with my body temperature and causing not only constant unbearable pain but scrambling my brain like it was an egg in a hot pan, I endured delirium and confusion, hallucinations so real I could touch them, vivid libidinous dreams that felt like flashbacks or memories of another life, not mine. I remember seeing men dancing topless in my bedroom; their glass bodies. Shame-faced, lanky and impure in heart, two handsome boys with long legs that are so shaped and tight that the best way to get at them is with the tongue. For the length of a moment I felt myself clad in steel. How far from me were my arm muscles. At one point I was the doctor from Kafka's tale, while another time I was the wounded patient wishing to die, or was I both simultaneously? I rolled around in jungled linen like the country doctor rolls around in bed with his patient, the young man with the wound the size of a plate in his side. I'm pretty sure at some point I was also both of the horses that transport the doctor, as well as being, briefly, also the stableboy, unhinged by lust, and then I was his victim, the terrified servant girl, Rosa, who shivers as I shivered, ached the same as me, knowing her fate and knowing her attempt at escape was futile. For those interminable days of tempest and ineffable agony I was totally unaware of the world outside my tiny room. I went for days without food, though water I could keep down.

Take off his clothes, then he will heal, someone said.

After the young man's family had undressed me and carried me, naked as sin, over to their son's sick bed and lain me against his wounded flesh, I felt more disoriented and lost in this erratic scribble of a life than ever. I looked into his indifferent eyes and said, 'Am I you or are you me?'

He pulled me close – the bed was very narrow – and the contact of our bodies was vertiginous. A caress arrived like the wind. Placing his unlucky lips upon my ear, he whispered, 'Don't bend; don't water it down; don't edit your own soul according to the fashion. Rather, follow your most intense obsessions mercilessly. There is ink, and there is blood. Perhaps the world doesn't really exist.'

Then I'm naked and pressed up against the young patient,

who's also naked. A naked young man is in the bed with me. How did he get here?

'Do you know,' I hear said into my ear, 'I came into this world with a beautiful wound.' He had a pleasant voice, and the proximity of his lips and his hot breath in my ear gave me an instant erection which I felt bat against his equally stiff and perky, though considerably larger, cock. My heart beat so fast I thought it would stop. The joy again of imagining a knife twisted in my heart. I found myself imagining in my febrile frenzy doing all sorts of piggy shit with this beautiful boy pressing his impressive member against mine and whispering in my ear, 'If my kiss offends you, avenge yourself and kiss me.'

I had several nocturnal emissions, all intense enough to wake me. Before falling asleep I felt on my body the weight of the fists on his light arms, obstructions in the throat. The soul flutters, the body trembles. A bird was in the room. These fragments of dreams, this stir of my subconscious, my tremulous private body, secretly yearning to cease to exist; the joy again of imagining a knife twisted in my heart. It can never be made good. The gaze that sees is a gaze that dominates. The unfettered force of truth. Is it true that doctors are the priests of the body? Was the boy in my bed circumcised or not?

My fur coat is hanging from the back of the door, but I can't reach it. I'm shivering so much I can't move, if that makes sense. I'm violently vibrating with involuntary movement and until it decides to release me from its spastic grip I can do nothing. The disappearance of voluntary movements and reduced activity. In disease one recognises life because it's on the law of life that knowledge of the disease is also based. At one point I found myself mumbling, the birth of the clinic is the death of the patient, over and over, with increasing insistence, as if I were trying to win an argument by sheer volume with an absent, fabricated interlocutor.

All this I've reported already to those who found me. This discourse already exists, somewhere. Contagion is the brute fact of the epidemic. A whole teratology of pathogens.

'You', I said, and gave him a little shove with my knee (at this sudden utterance some saliva flew from my mouth as an evil omen), 'don't fall asleep!'

I was planning to talk about how health doesn't seem to Kafka such an enviable possession. He would seem to agree with André Gide that health is 'merely an equilibrium, a state of mediocrity in everything; an absence of hypertrophies. Our value lies solely in what distinguishes us from others; idiosyncrasy is the disease that gives us that value; or in other words, what matters in us is what we alone possess, what can be found in no other, what your *normal man* lacks – hence what you call disease'*. Like Gide, Kafka is imploring us to stop looking upon disease as a deficiency, but rather as something additional: 'A hunchback is a man plus a hump'†, as Gide tells us. Illness sets you apart from the human race because it is the one true emblem of the human race.

In Kafka's tale, of course, the country doctor finds himself in bed with a young male patient who has a wound the size of a plate in his side, filled with blood-spattered, many-legged white worms writhing inside its open mouth; a wound made in a sharp corner with two blows of an axe, perhaps. The overwhelming fear of the queer body is one

---

*   Gide, André, *Cahiers 49/Notebooks*
†   Gide, André, *Cahiers 49/Notebooks*

of those ancient fears, adopted by Christians and never relinquished.

I'd prepared a rich multiverse of imagery to accompany and illustrate my talk, culled from the squalid cornucopia of the Mütter Museum, the Wellcome Library, the Royal College of Surgeons and the like: a panoply of vivid and visceral examples of illness as metaphor, a rogue's galleria of grotesqueries, deformities, hypertrophies, exquisite flowers of malady. I wondered, momentarily, if my endlessly researching and writing about sickness had precipitated this fevered spin of delirium under whose spell I conjured visions of such verisimilitude that I cannot claim to be able to separate the real from the imagined when I recount those few weeks in which I writhed like Margery Kempe or Saint Theresa in a St. Vitus Dance of ecstatic torture, or tortured ecstasy.

My paper argues that Kafka, in this story, looks upon health as a deficiency of disease, a precarious state for anyone that bodes no good. If we consider that two men sharing a bed, in Kafka's time, would be considered abnormal, a sickness, the story's message seems clear enough.

I was aiming to conclude by saying that the homosexual death drive comes *not* from homosexuals themselves, but from those *witnessing homosexuality*, who refuse to see in such behaviour anything but the horrendous desire for self-annihilation, negation, a reckless galloping towards death; for them, homosex signifies nothing but the very opposite of life. The cosmological values implicit in the Enlightenment are still at work here. Before the rise of so-called civilization, we had only the simplest, most necessary diseases, such as homosexuality, which passes from sin to sickness like a lava becoming its full-winged potentiality.

Kafka's queer optic sees the death drive as something to be embraced fervently till you expire in the arms of a beautiful man with a beautiful wound in his side the size of a plate, his outstretched leg in its grey rolled-up sock, that beautiful man in which, as with all beautiful men, homoeroticism lies encrypted. That beautiful wound is a sigil, something a healthy man lacks. Kafka, that poet of shame and guilt, clearly 'considered his homosexual orientation the best part of himself and the "indestructible element" in himself,'* as Tiefenbrun writes.

Kafka venerates the wound, the affliction, the sickness, the disease that gives him value.

The queer is thus a sagittal figure of knowledge, suturing two impossibilities. The queer body is both the wound and the stitching that helps your queer skin heal; both poison and cure: a pharmakon. Put your queer mouth against my queer face and let me switch on with that proximity. Let's fuck while your family stands there to witness the ineffable silence of our bodies.

Jonathan Kemp's debut novel *London Triptych* (Myriad, 2010) was acclaimed by the *Guardian* as an 'ambitious, fast-moving, and sharply written work' and by *Time Out* as 'a thoroughly absorbing and pacy read.' It was shortlisted for the inaugural Green Carnation Prize and won the Authors' Club Best First Novel Award in 2011. A story collection, *Twentysix* was published by Myriad in November 2011,

---

* Tiefenbrun, Ruth, *Moment of Torment: An Interpretation of Franz Kafka's Short Stories* (Southern Illinois University Press, 1973)

followed by a second novel, *Ghosting,* in March 2015. His first book of non-fiction, *The Penetrated Male*, was published by Punctum Books in 2012, with a second, *Homotopia? Gay Identity, Sameness & the Politics of Desire* in 2016. He has been teaching creative writing for twenty years and is currently at Middlesex University. He is putting the finishing touches to a new fiction, *Fiftytwo*, to be followed by a novel, *Neither/Nor,* and a collection of essays, *Not Dead Yet.*

Bo – Tom Spencer

I'm not even gay.
I'm not even a girl.
I just like to kiss boys and dress nice.

His fist collides hard with the back of my head. I didn't expect it, so I fall down straight away, almost smashing my face in on the gravel. I feel a kick aimed at my stomach but it misses by a couple of inches. It's still painful. A gob of spit lands next to me on the pavement. Before I can even register it, there's another thud on the ground. This time it's him, and my buddy Vic is on top of him, his arm pressed hard against the boy's chest. It's defensive. Not offensive. Vic's never on the offensive. He says he had to learn the hard way that he doesn't want to be on the offensive.

I sit up. Brad Marsh, the guy who clocked me, is swearing, lashing out, calling out to his mates. They don't come though. They had his back when he was going after me. Or when he was going after that Year Eleven. Not now though. Not now rugby star Victor King is involved.

'Fucking saddo,' I yell at him, cringing as I pull myself up. 'Picking on younger kids.'

We're in Year Thirteen. You don't hit kids. No excuse.
I turn towards the Year Eleven. I only know he's in Year
Eleven 'cause he's in my form. If I didn't know it, I'd think
he was in Year Nine or something. He's tiny.

'You all right?' I ask, touching the back of my head. It
smarts. Fucking saddo.

The kid nods. I try to remember his name. I can't. Hope
it's not from the head injury.

'Sorry, what's your name again?' I ask.

'Alfie,' he says. I notice his bag has a Batman logo on it.
I laugh and jab a thumb in Victor's direction.

'Guess you met a real superhero today, huh?'

It's cheesy but Alfie laughs. I slap him on the back and
tell him to get to class before a teacher comes. I also say if
this guy bothers him again, to tell us. He nods and starts
walking away. He doesn't say thank you but it doesn't
bother me.

'Get off me.' Brad finally manages to push Vic off but I
think it's only because Vic loosened his grip. I grin and lean
on Vic's shoulders. He's still on top of him and it's clear Brad
ain't gonna risk punching Vic.

'You gonna be bothering little 'uns again?' I ask, putting
on my best shit-eating grin.

'Fuck off!'

'See, that's not really the answer we're looking for,' Vic
grins. I laugh. We are superheroes. Bully busters. Proper
vigilante shit.

'What on Earth is going on here?'

Shit.

Mr O'Hara comes round the corner. Vic stands up so fast
I almost topple off the ground. Brad's mates scatter, leaving
us three standing around looking suspicious as.

'Nothing,' Brad answers, though looking at Vic like he'd really like nothing to be something. 'Just horsing around.'

'Yeah,' Vic says, putting an arm around Brad. Brad pushes it off. 'Just a bit of banter, you know how it is, sir.'

Vic can charm anyone. But Mr O'Hara sees my fucked up face and doesn't seem to bite.

'I'll try that again,' he says, looking at all three of us. 'What happened?'

'Kit fell,' Vic says. 'That's all it was.'

Brad nods and so do I. O'Hara scowls but he knows he's not gonna get anywhere.

'Go to class,' he says, 'and Brad don't forget you've got an after-school with me.'

Brad protests but O'Hara's not talking to us so we head off towards PE. As we turn the corner, Vic puts his arm around me and pulls me into a headlock. I start pushing and punching him and laughing.

'*What* are you two doing?'

Vic lets go and I back away to see Tabby catching up to us, smiling and shaking her head. Her make-up is on-point today. She's porcelain anyway, so she don't need any foundation but she does this great green eyeliner that looks absolutely top.

'Nothing,' I tell her shrugging as she comes between me and Vic, 'where were you? You didn't come to the common at break.'

'Lavender was helping me with my homework,' she says, as she reaches out for Vic's hand. He grabs it and gives her a kiss on the cheek. Fuck's sake.

'Lavender?' Vic asks. 'Who's that?'

'She's the girl who sits in front of us in Psychology,' I tell him. 'Brown hair, skinny, a bit—'

'*Don't say it,*' Tabby warns, glaring at me. 'What have you got now?' she asks, turning to Vic.

Vic tells her we have PE as I shove my hands in my pockets and look down on the ground. I don't get why Tabby has a go at me for stuff like that. She's always known I think Lavender's annoying. It's just description, innit?

When we get to the gym, Vic kisses Tabby goodbye. Not just a peck. They proper go for it. I'm not anti-public affection and that, but come on. It's mental. There're teachers around. I lock eyes with our PE teacher, Mr Arnould, who grins and rolls his eyes.

'See you, bubs,' Tabby says, kissing Vic one final time on the cheek. 'Bye, Bo.'

I don't say anything but I raise my eyebrows in response. Once she turns around, Vic puts his arm around me again.

'You're gonna have to talk to her sometime, you know,' he laughs.

Vic, mate. You don't get it. You don't get what it's like seeing someone kiss the person you've wanted all your life. You don't get what it's like knowing it's impossible to ever be with that person. You don't get what it's like being the other guy.

Fuck, I know I sound like that loser from *Love Actually*. But I can't help it.

I'm in love with Vic.

And I always have been.

*

'Are you wearing tights?'

I grin and laugh at Grayson. 'Nah, they're gym leggings.'

'You see, Gray,' Vic says, clapping me on the back. 'My boy here is a total fucking pussy.'

I tsk at Vic and shake my head. 'Nah, mate, I get eczema. My trousers rub.'

For some reason this is funnier so Vic and Grayson laugh harder. I just grin and take the banter. It's not like that's the real reason I do it anyway so no harm, no foul. Thing is, winter is the only time I can shave my legs really. No one expects you to wear shorts in the winter and no one is seeing any part of your legs. Only issue is PE so I wear these gym leggings.

As I sit down to pull on my trainers, I let a finger brush against my bald ankle. It feels well good. Like, I don't know why but when I've got hair on my legs I feel proper dirt. Almost like it's not me or something. I don't know the ins and outs of it but shaving my legs just makes me feel better and I feel like you should do what makes you feel better. You know, as long as it don't hurt no one and especially don't tell no one.

Vic claps his hands together, starts bouncing on the spot and hyping himself up. Grayson kisses the cross necklace he wears even though he doesn't believe in God. A few other boys do some stretching and all these other traditions they've seen footballers do. It makes me laugh. We're only doing PE. What difference is all this gonna make and what does it matter? I just stand up and walk outside the changing rooms, tapping the side of the door with my foot for good luck.

*

I can't describe how I feel as I look in the mirror. It's not like a sexual thing. I don't think it's even like a gender thing or whatever. I don't know what it is. But I really like looking in the mirror and seeing her on the other side. I'm wearing my neon pink wig which has black dip-dyes. My freckles are hidden beneath a layer of foundation and I have silvery eye-shadow around my black eye-liner eyes. The mascara makes my already long eyelashes look even longer. I pucker my black lipsticked lips and lean forward. I look so different.

I look, like, proper pretty. I sit down on my bed, away from my mirror, and cross my legs – picking up my phone. I'm not really all that into goth or scene stuff but I'm wearing a checkered skirt and fishnets because it looks amazing to be honest. I've got girl in red on my Spotify playlist although the next song is MCR. Emo shit, Grayson calls it. Tabby even thinks it's too heavy. I pretend I do too because it's easier than saying I like it. I wonder how many people do that.

My phone buzzes but it's just a snapchat from Tabby and will inevitably be her traditional group send to everyone saying how bored she is.

I open it up,

It is.

As always, I ignore it and lean back onto my bed.

I wonder what she would do if I sent her a selfie back – dressed like this – and was just like, 'me too'.

I smirk.

It'd be funny but I wouldn't.

Tabby would be so cringe about it too. She'd think I was gay and call me her gay best friend or think I'm *one of the girls*.

I'm not even gay.

I'm not even a girl.

I just like to kiss boys and dress nice.

We don't need to put labels on everything. I just want to be me and being me includes me at school and her in the mirror.

I check the time. It's almost five. My dad will be home soon and my mum shortly after him. Sighing, I stand up and spin one final time in the mirror to see my skirt twirl. Then, I fiddle with a curl on my wig and I smile.

Back in the box you go.

Just as I bend over to get my chest, the music I was listening to is interrupted by the sound of my alarm. I look over towards my phone, confused. I didn't set an alarm. Why would I? As I get closer, my phone background has been changed to a picture of Vic. I bite my lip.

He's calling me.

Also, shit I have lipstick on my teeth.

I pick up my phone and answer.

'All right, mate?' I say. He doesn't usually call me. In fact, outside of a couple of texts here and there, we're not really phone friends. We see each other every day so why would we be?

'Nah,' Vic says. 'My step-dad is being a prick again. Is it alright if I crash at yours?'

'No,' I say quickly, feeling my stomach drop. There's silence at the other end of the phone and I realise what that just sounded like. 'Wait, I mean, yeah. Sorry, I got confused. When are you getting here?'

I quickly pull off my thigh-highs and start pulling down my skirt.

'Are you all right?' Vic asks. 'I mean, I can see if I can crash at Grayson's instead?'

Part of me thinks about it. For a millisecond, I think

about saying I'm too busy. But the main bit of me, the loud bit of me, wants to see him this evening.

'Nah, come round mine,' I say quickly. 'Just, what time will you be here?'

'I'm just round the corner now,' he says. 'What's your Mum cooking tonight? It's not gonna be a bother, is it?'

Fuckfuckfuckfuckfuckfuckfuckfuckfuckfuckshitfuck

I kick off my skirt and rip off my wig.

'Bo?'

I quickly pull over my jumper and I start shoving it all in my chest. Then I grab a make-up wipe.

'Bo?'

Fuck this. I hang up on him. He'll understand. I'll just say I was wanking or some shit. I look in the mirror and start wiping. Fucking make-up won't come off. Fucking idiot, why black? Why the fuck did I choose black?

It's in my teeth.

How the fuck do I get it off my fucking

The front door opens.

He doesn't have a key. I didn't hear the bell? How did he?

'– 'course it's no bother, Vic,' my dad's voice comes from downstairs. 'With Frankie at uni, Pauline usually makes an extra plate anyway. Habit. Plus, you spend so much time here, we may as well adopt—'

WHY THE FUCK WOULD DAD COME HOME EARLY TODAY

I wipe hard and start grabbing at my uniform, pulling on my trousers first then throwing on the T-shirt I wore underneath my shirt today. There are footsteps coming up the stairs and a knock at the door.

'Robert, mate,' my Dad says, 'Vic's here.'

I KNOW VIC'S HERE YOU TWAT

'All right,' I say, 'cheers.'

My chest is still out and I haven't had time to lock it. I throw it in the wardrobe. I can lock it up when Vic's taking a shower or something.

The door opens. Vic steps in. The curtains are closed, my music is still playing and my clothes are all over the floor. Vic steps into the room, eyebrows raised and closes the door behind him.

'You wanking or something?'

He opens the curtains and turns to look at me.

His smile falters.

His brilliant smile falters and his deep brown eyes look me up and down as if X-raying me or something.

And my first thought is – I feel fucking sick.

And my second thought is – what have I missed?

I turn to look in the mirror.

A huge black smudge beside both eyes, a foundation spot on my right cheek and two black lipstick dots on my bottom lip. I look at the floor. Make-up wipes.

Make-up wipes and a pink and black striped thigh-high sock.

I swallow.

Vic drops his bag.

Vic's not homophobic. He's not transphobic. He doesn't think men have to dress like men or that men should only kiss women.

He's a feminist.

He once did a charity run for LGBTQ+ kids.

He posted pro-trans shit on Twitter almost daily when some celebrity he liked spoke out against trans people a few years ago.

He's a good guy, Vic.

I shift uncomfortably, pick up my make-up wipes and carry on wiping. I watch myself in the mirror as I do it. Making sure I get everything.

Vic walks forward, picking up my sock.

He starts to say something but I don't quite hear it and he gives up halfway through. I want to run away. I want to punch something.

I take a deep, shaky breath – turn to him, now clean-faced and take the sock off him.

'Don't tell no one,' I say.

'I won't,' he says, his voice sounding crackly.

'I mean it,' I say and suddenly something roars inside me and I hate how he's looking at me. Looking at me like he feels sorry for me or is worried about me or something. His eyes wide. His mouth open. I walk forward and grab him by the shirt.

I grab him by the shirt and I know it must look like a fucking joke because I'm so much smaller than him.

'I'm not fucking gay,' I say and I don't know why.

'I didn't say you were,' Vic says, swallowing.

'I'm not,' I whisper.

'I know,' he whispers back.

'I just—' I say but something large in my throat stops me from finishing the sentence.

Vic is looking in my eyes. I feel hot tears start streaming down. He presses a thumb against my cheek and wipes one away.

'It's OK,' he whispers.

'This doesn't mean anything,' I manage.

'It doesn't *change* anything,' he whispers back. Then he bites his lip. He's looking at me. Studying me. We've been this close before but I've never felt this. What's happening? Why's this happening? Why did he have to come now?

He leans forward.

I feel his lips press against mine.

I pull him closer and kiss back.

We only part after we hear the front door open again and my mum call up a hello. We call back down a hello and sit down on the bed. It's awkward. His knee is tapping against mine.

'I bet —' he says, rubbing the back of his head. His hand inches towards mine.

What do you want to say, Vic?

Tell me what you want to say.

'I bet you look beautiful,' he tells me, looking me dead in the eyes.

I feel my mouth break into a grin and I start crying again. Feeling like a pussy. After he gets me back together, he says it again. He says he bets I look beautiful.

'I'll show you,' I say, nodding. 'Later, when they've gone to sleep, I'll show you.'

He smiles. Smiles that amazing fucking smile.

I don't like labels. I don't think we need them. I don't think I'm gay or nothing.

But maybe I am.

Is there anything wrong with it?

No.

Of course not.

Because I guess it doesn't change anything.

Vic reaches forward and holds my hand.

I don't know who I am.

I don't know what I am yet.

I'm only seventeen.

Maybe I am gay.
Maybe I'm a girl.
Maybe I just like to dress nice and kiss boys.
But there's one thing I know right now.
Right now in this moment.
He leans forward again.
And kisses me.

Tom Spencer is a Winchester-based writer, wonderfully enamoured by the story of the underdog. He has been published in various literary magazines and has been hard at work, polishing his manuscript.

The Only Thing I Accept is Despair* – Piero Toto

I've spun a quilt with wounds
& trimmed your alphabet anew

our names *never to exist again*
buried by parents white as distance

all blood made into ribbons
stitched into cloth
       into sonnets that shout
mine is the last voice you'll hear

over time I've learnt
to trust saliva as it dries

---

*   The Only Thing I Accept is Despair is a line from Rainer Werner
Fassbinder's *Beware of a Holy Whore* (1971); the poem contains snippets
from the UK AIDS Memorial Quilt Project [2021].

Piero Toto (he/him) is a London-based bilingual poet, Italian translator and translation lecturer at London Metropolitan University. His poems in English have appeared in *fourteen poems*, *Queerlings* and *harana poetry* amongst other publications; his debut Italian poetry pamphlet, *tempo 4/4* (Transeuropa Edizioni, 2021), was longlisted in the International Mario Luzi Poetry Prize 2021. Twitter/Instagram: @pierototoUK.

Talking to Ghosts on Geary St. –
Marilyn Smith

Will you be cold up there on that Cumbrian fell? When the wind roars down the tumbling green flanks to butt the drystone graveyard walls and shake the yew tree from its dreaming. Will my secret still reach you? My sordid little secret, so a vicious ex-friend once spat. Would it shock you? Disappoint you? Would you worry about what people think? Always what people think. You're resting now under the heart-stone. A semi-quaver etched upon its face, my gentle nod to your silenced voice. And then there's the matter of your name. The maiden name of a brave young woman who once sang upon a Northern stage while the sea churned mud-brown beneath a seaside pier. The curtain fell for the final time as the wedding ring slid on, but the music still played in your head. So, you sang in the kitchen, soft black curls falling from your headscarf as you rolled out your pastry. You sang me to sleep, lit only by the yellow landing light that fell through my childhood bedroom door. And you sang in the darkened stalls watching others take your place as I cringed into my bag of sweating toffee eclairs. A lifetime of compliance. Stay in lane. Marry a man, have children. Take the smallest slice of cake. Make the men a drink. Be kind, smile, get smaller and smaller and always put your lipstick on. Until now that is. You waited under the cover of death to stage your rebellion. Make sure you put my maiden name on the gravestone, you said. Not his name. *Mine.* And so I did, glad I'd never argued that your maiden name didn't belong to you either. A man owned that too.

At David's on Geary, it's seating room only at the bar. Sipping bitter coffee with a belly full of breakfast burrito I bring you back to life in Northern California. Remember I brought you here once? I resurrect you on the cable car inching up from Market Street. *Ding ding ding went the trolley* you sing, and I laugh. We ascend. Climbing up and up, leaving behind the piss-stained drunks and the spice addicts and the red-faced angry man who tells us God hates Gays. Turn to Jesus and be saved. I turn to you and see your shining widowed face as the Bay reveals itself at the top of Van Ness. Descending past parks of pensioners doing Tai Chi and self-conscious coffee shops, we see Alcatraz white stoned under an April sun. I think of the sharks in the water. There is no escape even if you make a leap for freedom. Maybe only the Birdman was able to soar up into the cold blue sky when he was so inclined.

But I'm procrastinating, like I always do when I need to tell you something that makes my cheeks burn. Remember I couldn't even tell you about the bright-red stain that appeared in my knickers when I was ten. Or that I needed my first bra. You only placed a hand on my bony chest and frowned. Tell me if they start to hurt, you said. I never did. I went to Mothercare instead with my best friend Susan who held up two white lace triangles and pressed them to my teenage chest. Later she would press herself against me on her parent's bed and put her fingers inside me. I never told you about that either. But it's different now. It's time we talked. Death robbed us of this moment. Some would say that was a blessing. And yet, I wonder. I picture you sitting next to me here at the bar. The waitress has clucked over to refill my cup. The noisy chatter and the hiss and froth of the coffee machine seems to grow louder, and the windows are steaming up a treat. I'm glad I don't have to face you. I can look ahead and watch our reflections in the speckled glass. Deep breaths. Here I go.

'Mam, I'm in love.'

It sounds ridiculous to voice it, especially to the ghost of you. I squirm on the bar stool. Can we talk about the weather instead? Like we used to when we wanted to avoid talking. We're on safer ground there. Your face breaks into a smile in the mirror.

'I'm glad for you daughter. Are you happy?'

I lift my cup to my mouth with both hands, and I sip to buy some time. This is it. The truth. Le noble truth. Nothing but the truth. So help me gay-hating God.

'Happy? Yes, I'm happy.'

Bright red. My face flushes. Just like it did when the nuns made the boys hold hands with the girls. Boy, girl, boy, girl. First Holy Communion. Little miniature brides and grooms in white and black, singing *Ave Maria* in thin falsetto voices as we walked in shy procession up the church steps. Above us apple blossom stretched across a Manchester sky, petals falling to the ground when the breeze rustled through.

'I'm in love with a woman, and her name is like a melody.'

You go quiet. Like I knew you would. I can't bear to look at you. Did we ever really know each other, Mam? I glimpsed you briefly before the end when you finally spoke up for yourself. I just stare into my cup, and I think of her as you stay silent. The glow of the bedside alarm clock lighting her beautiful face as she rises before me. The champagne bottle empty on the carpet and the last Metro long departed, we pull back the soft sheets and slip inside. Her blue eyes are wide open. Watching me. She who buries her face in my hair and breathes in the skin of my neck to read my emotions. Fear, euphoria, pain, happiness. You name it, she has caused them all.

I feel your hand close over mine. How is it so warm?

'My daughter, you summoned me here to tell me about the woman you love. What is it you want? My blessing? My approval? My dismay?'

I stare down at some stains on the countertop.

'Not sure what I want. To share this with you, I guess. To tell you about her. Would you have been happy for us? It's all too late now.'

Your laugh surprises me. Its lightness and its depth.

'Do you think this is news to me, daughter? Do you think I no longer sense you? When you stand in the Mediterranean shallows, your lips on hers as tiny fish nibble your calves. When you scour a Breton beach for the clams she cooks for you, do you not know I feel the warmth of the hot August sand beneath your feet and your trembling hand in hers?'

'You can see us?' I start.

'No daughter, I can feel you. There are no secrets. No shame, no disapproval, no judgement, no regrets. This is what I know now. There is only love.'

I look up into the speckled mirror to see your face. You have disappeared. I see only myself staring back. The space beside me is empty but I am filled with peace.

Marilyn Smith is a writer of short stories and flash fiction, and a proud contributor to the *QLQL* anthologies. When not daydreaming or sky surfing, she lives in Paris with her beloved *Cheffe* in a neighbourhood where they walk on rainbows to cross the streets.

She Sleeps – William Wyld

she sleeps with grit between her teeth she sleeps beneath
a half-opened parachute she lies
across two beds at once she sleeps in the street

she sleeps by the open window sleeps below
drifts of snow sleeps with a black bow
tied around her neck she sleeps on bare springs
and in wet wool at sea on deck she sleeps
in an inch of water

she sleeps with her eyes open and her face covered
kicking up the sheets like a marquee in a thunderstorm
she sleeps through thunderstorms
she sleeps on her belly in the rain on the grass
she sleeps so close you can't move

she sleeps on her feet she sways
back and forth on the quay
in time with the swell of the sea
and she sleeps where she falls

prone prostrate, curled in a ball
balanced on the sea-sucked edge of the harbour wall

she sleeps in her coat, sleeps with wet hair
sleeps through dreams of talking fish
forest fires and nightmares
salt water welling up in her throat
and she wakes and she slips downstairs
and out to sleep up on the high moor
beneath the ponies' feet and the cries of jackdaws
she sleeps to beat the creeps that try to rip
the small bones of power from her claws

and she sings
she sings as she sleeps
she sings of things the ocean brings in frozen heaps
the slick black sheaths of kelp
the seals trapped in nets she cannot help
that swell and rot on the beach

and she sleeps in the pelts she keeps
that reek of the gulls that circle' shriek
and dive if you're fool enough to breach
the precincts of their rude nests that lie
high on the tide line drenched by sheets
of late spring rain and she cries

she cries out in grief as she sleeps
and it's not for you to lift the sheet from her wet cheek
and it's not for you to speak
your time is brief
and she's not here to listen to you weep

William Wyld. Raised by a couture dress designer, cos-
tume and identity have always been central to William's
writing. He has performed poetry at Wilderness Festival
and the Saison Poetry Library, appeared in the *Live Cannon
Sonnet Anthology* and the *Lighthouse Journal*, and been
shortlisted for the Troubadour international poetry prize.
William's background is in the visual arts; he has exhibited
at the Royal Academy Summer Show and Discerning Eye
exhibitions. A carpenter by trade, he is currently helping
rebuild the Museum of Childhood in Bethnal Green

To a Moustache – Martha Benedict

To feel you there above my lips
Highlighted by the golden, paling light
My jawline, cut sharp, as the sunset dips
My face shapeshifts, once more – the onset of night

In the darker hours my mind wanders free
To wonder: how would my face feel?
To appear: handsome, dandy, unabashed

Looking in the mirror – choosing not to flee
Fully formed: gentlemanly, debonair, genteel
My face. Finally . . . finely moustached.

Martha is an emerging writer, DJ, dancer and artist currently studying an MA in The Poetics of Imagination. She can often be found wherever there is good company, music, food and dancing – whether that's in a field or someone's front room! Some of her influences include Kae Tempest, Eddie Izzard and their own lived, liminal experiences as a creative queer person. artscontent.substack.com

Love and Oranges – Finn Brown

Toni

'This isn't dark. The sky's barely purple. Real darkness is purple,' says Greta when I tell her I am afraid of the dark.

I am lying on my front, but I roll over onto my back so I can look at the sky through Greta's eyes. To me it looks dark, nothing more. 'I think you see more colours than other people do,' I say.

Greta puts her ear to her shoulder. I can't see her expression, but I know she is smiling. She likes that kind of compliment. 'Other people just aren't looking,' says Greta and now I hear the smile in her voice too. 'Give me your little finger. Go on.' I hold it up. 'Most of it's a sort of rusty orange. Pink at the tip, but your nail is white on the edges, purple at the base. A cherry plum purple. You know the sort. All that shadow around your knuckle. There's blue in there too and when you flex it like that it goes yellow before it goes white.' I hold my hand against the sky and see only my skin against darkness.

'You amaze me.'

'Being colour blind is one of my worst fears. Waking up one day to grayscale.'

I sit up because Greta doesn't usually talk about her fears. I do. I talk about them all the time. Not Greta. 'What are the others?' I say, even though I expect I am pushing my luck.

'Other what?'

'Fears.'

'Oh.' Greta looks down at her hands and I wonder what colours she is seeing and whether she will slap me for asking questions she knows I know she doesn't like to answer.

'You don't have to—' I say guiltily, but she interrupts.

'Rape. Childbirth. Losing my mind. Losing you.' There is a very long silence which seems to stretch like skin over bones. 'You have thought about it, haven't you?'

'Yes,' I say. This is true. I have thought about leaving my husband for her since the day that I met her. I have thought about it even more since the day that she asked me to.

'So,' says Greta.

Again, we wait. Two sirens speed past, rising and falling just out of time, the matching sounds jarring. A boy screams in the distance, a happy scream full of adrenaline. Teenagers playing.

'How can I?' I say, eventually.

'How can you not?' says Greta.

'What would people say?' I ask, and I hate myself for saying it because of the person that it makes me.

Greta puts my face in her hands. 'We'll go to a place without people. Just you, me and the kids. It's good for kids to see the world. It's good for you to see the world. I'll find you a corner of the world where all you can see in every direction is sun on water. We'll swim naked wherever we go and in winter we'll keep each other warm with our breath. Say yes. You must say yes to that.'

I stand up because if I don't I will kiss Greta. 'They need to go to school,' I say. 'They need to be with people their own age.'

Greta stands up too. 'Then we'll move to Manchester, Birmingham. I'd even settle for Leeds – that's how much I love you.'

'Lola needs to be with her dad.'

'No.'

I turn away from Greta because I am aching in my stomach. If I had not spent so much time around sickness in the last few months I would've called a doctor for an ache like that. 'He's dying, Greta. You should see his skin, it's the colour of limes. That's how you'd describe it. They've put this spit-blue curtain around him to hide his shrinking limbs from the families of the other dying men. The other night we could see fireworks out of the window that were brighter than his face. And he looked at me so sad and I looked back, all anger. Because here I am, wanting this thing that is bigger than the earth, and there he, is dying.'

'Bigger than the earth?' says Greta, who is crying.

'He's dying,' I say again because – after all – these are the words I am choosing over 'I love you.' I put my hand to her face and I push the tears to her hairline with my thumb. She takes my hands away from her face and looks at both of them, then at me.

'I ought to go,' she says. She stands up and rearranges her jumper around her hips. She looks forward like her eyes are meeting a horizon. Then she starts walking away.

265

'Wait. Couldn't you wait? Wait for him to be better. Wait for him to die. Either way I'll come with you then.'

'I promised myself I would never wait for a woman to be ready to leave her husband again,' says Greta, facing away from me towards the swimming pool. I think about drowning.

'Where will you go?' I ask.

'I'll see you, maybe,' she says, without moving.

I think about water like a weight on my chest, I think about breathing it in, limbs thrashing. 'Tell me where you're going,' I say over and over again, long after she has disappeared behind the swimming pool, long after the sound of teenagers has died, long after the sky has turned purple.

*

'That is how you lose things,' Greta says to me one day when I drop a segment of orange and do not pick it up until I have eaten the rest. There is juice on my chin. We are in her kitchen. We do not go to my kitchen because my kitchen is not my own, and anyway the light in here is always softer. Greta's hair looks soft. It is longer than it was when I first met her, and it curls over her cheek. Her hair reminds us that we have been doing this a while.

'What's there to lose?' I say. 'There are orchards of oranges around the world. Imagine how that must smell, Greta. Imagine lying in an orchard of oranges and between you and the sky there's just orange and green, and the grass underneath you is stained with juice.'

'There's always something to lose,' says Greta.

I am still thinking about oranges. 'Brazil. China. Spain. We could chase orchards around the world. Where's the notebook?' Greta is looking out of the window and the back of her head looks strangely shaped, with all that light coming at it.

I open drawers until I find it, and write 'Orchards of Oranges' in blue biro at the end of a long list. I doodle an orange segment, looking half at the paper and half at the back of Greta.

'There's no point writing it down,' she says. 'We never leave the house.' Greta turns around and her eyes are glassy. She holds up one hand and her wrist looks very small, bone-like.

I go to her and catch it in the air. 'Are you unhappy?'

'I think I will be soon,' she says. 'Don't they ever wonder where you are?'

'Lola's a teenager. I spend far more time wondering where she is than she does wondering where I am. She won't tell me the names of her friends. She meets them after school and I don't know what they do together. Sometimes I drive around Lewisham looking for them. I don't find them.' I think about Lola's face, which is still stuck between childhood and adulthood, bones and puppy fat creating strange shadows.

'I was never that kind of mother.'

'They'd be friends, I think. Your child and mine,' I say. I imagine a teenager I have never seen with my own.

'Not when you have a husband,' says Greta and Ryan's face is in front of my eyes. Greta comes towards me. She walks slowly and stands very close to me. I can feel her breath on my cheek. She says, 'Will you ever leave him, Toni? Will you, though?'

'I—'

'There's always something to lose,' she repeats. Then

Greta scrapes the orange peel off the side and puts it in the bin.

Greta

I walk away from Toni even though she is calling my name. I walk past the swimming pool which is lit up, all bright and white and blue against the night. A lifeguard in yellow sits high-up, watching bodies, making sure they stay close enough to the surface. There aren't many people inside: several people swimming lengths, someone getting ready to dive, two women chatting on the steps with their ankles submerged. One touches the other's thigh and I wonder if they are lovers, then I realise they are giggling at the lifeguard.

I see queerness everywhere these days. I see Toni everywhere.

I keep walking. I don't know anything other than that I can't be here anymore.

I go to Kath's flat, which we used to share, and call her when I am outside. She opens the door in a blue dressing gown, wet hair down the side of her face. I follow her into the kitchen where she makes me tea. The radio is playing, an old love song that I recognise from my childhood, can hum along to but couldn't name. When the tea is brewed, we go down the hall and sit on her bed.

'So,' she says to me.

The tea is a Jasmine Green, soft and hot in my mouth. 'It's my heart,' I say.

'It always is,' says Kath. She looks tired, tired out by life and tired out by me. She takes moisturiser off the side table and dots it across her skin, then begins to circle it into her cheeks, her forehead, her chin.

'I think I need to go away for a bit.'

'You know what I am going to say Greta,' says Kath. Her face is shining now.

'This one is different. I really thought—'

'They never leave their husbands. Remember that,' says Kath, who also knows that this is true. 'Look, you can go away, disappear until you feel better. But remember that you have a teenager here who needs both parents. Me and you. Come back, that's all I'm asking. I know you find it hard. But come back.' Kath strokes my face. The first time I fell in love after Kath and I had separated, Kath was not this kind. I had disappeared to Scotland for months when our child was only five, and she was angry. A decade on and Kath has given up on me being dependable. All she asks, each time, is that I come back. I nod. I give her a hug. I make her a promise.

We finish our tea and then I turn out the lights. 'I'll wash up the cups on my way out,' I say to Kath as I close the door.

I know the kitchen well enough not to turn the light on. I feel my way through the space, over tiles and to the sink. The water washes over my hands as I scrub.

'Are you going again, Mum?' The voice comes from behind me as the kitchen light, glaring, turns on.

I shake my head, then I sit down. My fifteen-year-old sits down too, pulling their legs up into their chest. They look at me. I nod.

'Thought so,' they say. They tug at their ear.

'Careful,' I say. The ears are newly pierced, a weekend trip to Claire's Accessories that we had taken together two weeks ago. I go to the sink and wait for the water to get so hot I can't touch it anymore. Then I fill a mug and pour in salt. 'Here,' I say. I slide my body behind my child's and dab around each piercing with a dampened kitchen towel.

'It's hot,' they say.

'It's supposed to be.' I am very close to their ear so I speak quietly like they are much younger and I am trying to get them to sleep. 'You've got to do this every night, remember? That way the skin will heal. Promise me you'll remember?'

'Yes, Mum,' they say. 'I promise.' I stroke their hair. 'Plait it?'

I nod into their neck. 'How's school?' I ask as I begin to wind the hair.

'School is all right. I'm thinking about trying out for the football team. They get to wear sports kit in whatever class they have before practice, and if there's one thing I hate – I mean HATE, Mum – it's the new skirt-length rules. Am I a student or a nun? I might write an article titled that for the school paper. Do you think it's a good title, Mum?'

'Yes.' I tie a green hair band around one plait and move onto the other side of the hair.

'I'll have to do it, like, this weekend though, because Mandy Johnson said she wanted to write something about it. But I bet she won't have a title like that. Will she, Mum?'

'No,' I say. I listen to the way my child says 'mum'. They always do this, when they know I am leaving. Mum, they say, mum mum mum. They are telling me they still need me. This is always the moment where I think about stay-ing, but there is an ache growing in me like rot. And these things are better dealt with alone. I tie an orange band around the second plait and then wind my arms around their body. 'I'll miss you,' I say.

'Then why are you going?' they ask me.

I kiss the back of their ear and get up from the chair. 'Come on, I'll tuck you in.'

'How old do you think I am?' they say. They launch out of the kitchen and slam the door behind them.

A light is flashing in the stairwell as I come down from the flat. I wonder why it hurts so much to be left. I wonder why I am leaving.

Toni

Material billows around Greta. The smock is long and black (of course) and wide, and filled with breeze as she opens the door to me. She has woollen socks on her feet. Her hair sits just above her ears, shorter than when I last saw her. She leads me down a corridor covered in photographs and into her flat, which is small and covered in colour. There is a purple sofa and a small dining table with yellow chairs next to the mint kitchen. Through a white curtain pulled across the space I can see the shape of a bed, boxy furniture, and clothes hanging.

'Home,' says Greta, spreading one arm out. She makes tea and I touch things (books, a snow globe, long candles that don't match). Outside the window I can see sky and the top floors of other blocks of flats. Someone on a balcony is watering their plants. A child between their legs is biting a plastic tractor.

When I turn around Greta is behind me. She is holding a mug in each hand and steam rises from both. I take one and realise we are stood very close to each other. 'Sugar?' asks Greta. I shake my head.

We sit on the sofa with our knees touching. 'It's lovely,' I say about the flat. 'The photos, the colours.'

'I haven't been here long. A few months. I chose it for the colours. Sometimes I forget how much colour exists in the world. Not here.'

I think about my own kitchen, which is beige with a silver hob and black handles on the cupboard doors. We chose it because it was clean and timeless. We said these words to each other: clean, timeless. The salesman told us it would make our home easier to sell. People like a blank canvas, he said. I move closer to Greta.

'And the view,' I say. 'The sky.' It is blue today.

'Yes,' says Greta. 'Light.' Greta moves closer to me. We both look down at our mugs of tea and move them around in our palms.

'I took the bus here and the light through the front windows was almost blinding. I had to close my eyes, but I could still feel the light on my eyelids.' I close my eyes and feel the tips of Greta's fingers touch my eyelids.

'Here?' she asks. Her voice is close to my mouth. Her fingers touch my forehead and my temples and my cheeks, down the line of my nose, around my mouth, my ear lobes, my neck.

I open my eyes and I kiss Greta. It is me who kisses her. It is the only thing I can think of to do.

When we open our eyes again Greta stands up. She walks towards the white curtain and holds it open. A bed, a desk, a wardrobe. The walls are white apart from the left wall which is dark orange and green.

'I painted that,' she says.

I touch the wall. I run my hands over the ridges of the paint.

'Come here,' she says.

She takes off my clothes first. I feel her cool fingers on my stomach. Then I pull the smock over her head, and she is only wearing pants underneath.

We stand with our bodies very close together.

Later, Greta has turned small lights on all around the flat as the natural light has faded. We showered earlier, and then had sex again, so our hair smells like conditioner but our bodies smell of sweat. I am running my fingers around Greta's areolas.

She is laughing at me.

She says it is strange to see a woman my age touch another woman's areolas for the very first time.

Finn Brown's short stories 'Heat' and 'The Girl Who's Scared of Water' were published in *Transforming Being* and *The Bombay Review* respectively. They are currently editing a manuscript written whilst on the Creative Writing MFA at Birkbeck. They have performed poetry at Hay Festival, Last Word Festival and Brainchild Festival, and run an arts and literary platform called t'ART.

Miss Claire – Virna Teixeira

the scissors shaping the fabric
the textures and the tone
of this fantasy

too fluid this
delicate chambermaid
of the parallel rooms

how swiftly she moves
in the romantic rustle
of PVC and lace

treading softly with her
patent leather shoes
between corridors and textiles

camouflaged behind
the servile *senhorita*
sitting decorous

like the boy she carries
inside, so polite
in the waiting rooms of time

designing interiors
almost mummified
by invisible bondage tapes

Virna Teixeira is a Brazilian poet, translator, short story writer and visual artist based in London. Her last collection of poems, *My Doll and I* explores issues around crossdressing, gender, fantasy and power. She is the editor of *Theodora* zine and Carnaval Press. Her first book of short stories, *A Pupila*, was published in Brazil in 2022.

The Night We Met – Isabel Costello

The night we met in that gay bar
down some steps, beneath the neon sign
I could hear nothing but your voice
over the music blaring.
I could focus on nothing
but your blue eyes blazing
in a nightmare sea
of plastic flowers and Barbie dolls.

You said this one little thing, seriously,
and I knew then. I just knew.
Already I could imagine our endless conversations
about cities and books and narcissistic mothers.
About how complicated it is
to want different and incompatible things
that it pays to dare for
when we could all die tomorrow or choose to live.

I couldn't have anticipated
the feeling of your fingers inside me,
our skin and sounds fusing.

If you'd asked, I'd have said my dream was
to take you to Paris,
go down on you to the sound of church bells ringing
or something wild like that,
when the truth is as simple as this.

Isabel Costello is the author of two novels, *Paris Mon Amour* and *Scent*. Her short fiction has appeared in many anthologies. She is a creative writing tutor and mentor and runs the popular Literary Sofa blog. Isabel lives in London and has lifelong connections with France.

this is a ghost story –
Brian Thorstenson

two mugs of coffee on a formica table
a one block alley with its own police code
midnight: a set of weary footsteps
a small blue car goes missing
on the corner, an upstairs dance floor, filled with dykes,
is swallowed by the sky, or by the sea, a flying dream
a bar loses its flags and its gold shimmer curtains
another loses all its women
a bookstore, a cafe, a day spa
xeroxed posters appear on telephone poles
last seen, call if, missing:
queers, dykes, drag queens and trans folks
at 3 a.m. on 21st street the sound of showers
and moaning men hovers the sidewalk
a woman, in the back of a store, puts away
her beans, best in the city, her rice and tortillas,
her metal cash box, and locks the front door for the
      last time
a guidebook goes out of print

photographs and newspaper clippings whisper secrets
inside white cardboard boxes on black metal shelves
thursday, a five alarm fire, another saturday, a one alarm
    monday,
then a tent, two cars, a plywood box home
turn a corner or stop to tie shoelaces
faces float into peripheral view
some of them are singing show tunes
some of them are speaking spanish
some of them just stare and stare and stare
the small blue car wanders south

Brian Thorstenson is a San Francisco-based writer and teacher. His last series of projects included *Dearly Gathered* with choreographers Rowena Richie, Christy Funsch and Chris Black, and *Fugue* with Detour Dance. His poetry has appeared in *Foglifter*, Burning House Press, *Lambda Literary Review* and *New American Writing*. He is a Senior Lecturer at Santa Clara University.